Aftershocks

Books in English by Grete Weil

TRANSLATED BY JOHN S. BARRETT

The Bride Price
a novel

Last Trolley from Beethovenstraat
a novel

Aftershocks
stories

These are Verba Mundi Books,
published by David R. Godine

GRETE WEIL

Aftershocks

Stories

Translated from the German
by John S. Barrett

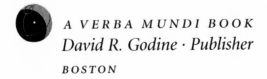

A VERBA MUNDI BOOK
David R. Godine · Publisher
BOSTON

This is a Verba Mundi Book, published in 2008 by
DAVID R. GODINE · *Publisher*
Post Office Box 450, Jaffrey, New Hampshire 03452
www.godine.com

The seven stories published here in English for the first time were originally written in German and first appeared in collections of Grete Weil's short fiction. The earliest item, "Finish What You Started," was published in 1968 in *Happy, sagte der Onkel* ("Happy, Said My Uncle," Limes Verlag, Wiesbaden); it was reprinted posthumously, in 1999, in *Erlebnis einer Reise* ("Account of a Journey," Verlag Nagel & Kimche, Frauenfeld, Switzerland). The remaining six stories make up the complete contents of *Spätfolgen* ("Aftershocks," Verlag Nagel & Kimche, 1992) and appear here in the order the author gave them. "The House in the Desert" is Weil's late revision of her story "Happy, Said My Uncle."

The translator and publisher wish to thank Verlag Nagel & Kimche for permission to include "Finish What You Started" among the stories in *Aftershocks.*

LIBRARY OF CONGRESS CATALOGING-IN-PUBLICATION DATA
Weil, Grete, 1906–1999
[Spätfolgen. English]
Aftershocks : stories / Grete Weil ; translated from the German by John S. Barrett. — 1st American ed.
p.   cm. — (Verba Mundi book)
Originally published: Zürich : Nagel & Kimche, 1992.
ISBN 978-1-56792-282-0
I. Title.
PT2647.E4157 6813 2008
833´.914—dc22
2008019741

First Edition
PRINTED IN CANADA

Contents

Introduction

For those born afterward, it seems almost inconceivable that anyone would be able to present the sufferings of the Holocaust in any coherent literary form. Where to begin? How to begin, when confronted by the sheer numbers of the victims of that devouring monster of human devising and the territory and time over which it roamed? But, incredibly, many of its survivors did know how and where to begin. Among them is Grete Weil, honored for the intellectual and emotional breadth of her fictional portrayals of that terrible epoch and its aftermath.

Weil began her efforts at literary witness after returning to Germany in 1947. After feeling her way back into writing by translating contemporary English works, including those of Lawrence Durrell and John Hawkes, she struck out on her own. One can imagine her gathering, subduing, and ordering the memories of her experiences with the Holocaust: the deceptive and short-lived safety of the Netherlands, the murder of her husband, her own eventual successful concealment, and her attempts to ensure her mother's survival until the war's end. One can see her walking around the smoldering remains of the beast, trying to think back to when it was whelped, how it grew, reminding herself of its appearance when alive, and watching the assembled image change when seen from a different perspective. The novels and short stories she produced reflect those journeys into memory and questioning, relating to each other and the central theme of the Holocaust like individual movements of a string quartet.

The leitmotif for *Aftershocks* was sounded in Weil's novel *Last Trolley from Beethovenstraat*, published just a few years earlier. The protagonist, Andreas, a budding German poet turned war correspondent, comes into contact with the Holocaust by accidentally witnessing the nighttime deportations of Dutch Jews, to which he reacts initially by thinking he is going insane. His postwar life is the answer to Theodor Adorno's question of whether anyone can write poetry after Auschwitz: Andreas cannot. His talent is handcuffed by memories, his promise goes unfulfilled, and his life remains one of unhappiness, despite material comforts. Weil's narrator says of him – of all who escaped death at the monster's hands: "As yet Andreas does not know, knows it just as little as the victims of Hiroshima, that they who have gotten away with their lives are doomed." *Aftershocks* presents the stories of those whose survival represented only a momentary reprieve from suffering and even doom. In that sense, Weil could have titled the present volume *Radiation Sickness*, but instead chose the deceptively neutral word "*Spätfolgen*," that is, "*sequellæ*" or "aftereffects," thus echoing the many seemingly neutral words used by the Nazis to conceal their crimes.

But the radioactivity analogy holds: like the globe-circling fallout from Chernobyl, the black cloud of the Holocaust in Weil's *Aftershocks* reaches far and wide, exerting its malign influence on the victims, on those left alive in Europe and those who had seemingly escaped to safe places like New York or California, the latter location suggesting the translation's title. The Holocaust's aftereffects, as Weil portrays them, have no expiration date, reaching years later into professional as well as private lives, tarnishing success and thwarting attempts to find simple, human pleasure, sometimes with the sudden destructiveness of a buried bomb. One of the stories unambiguously details a suicide: as did Primo Levi, Jean Améry, and Paul Celan, the main character takes his own life years after the war's end, simply unable to survive the loss of his wife. Other stories, like that of the teenage Jewish girl found drowned in the Seine, are less straightforward. A woman who had found the girl a place to hide during the war spends her retirement trying to discover the story behind the girl's fate only to run aground on the question of whether she was betrayed or simply ran away during a bout of teenage rebelliousness, troublesome enough on its own, but fatal in the setting of the Holocaust. Two other stories, "Guernica" and "The House in the Desert," detail the distorted existences of men and women who escaped to America, unable to shed their previous German cultural heritage, yet equally unable to adapt to more than a caricature of an American life, even though, in one instance, a professionally and financially successful one. The characters are harshly, even perhaps uncharitably drawn, as they struggle with their guilt at having escaped or their partial, agonized Americanization.

In the final story in the collection "And I? A Witness to Pain," Grete Weil deals equally harshly with herself as she comes to realize that she was able to go on living simply because she had never actually been in a death camp. She questions her position of writing as a witness because she had not witnessed the worst, had not "gazed upon the head of the Medusa." A witness to the persecution she had been, yes, but not to the actual deportations, and certainly not to the horrors of the concentration camps within one of which her husband was murdered. The story is so permeated by the author's despondency that the reader is likely to feel considerable gratitude that Weil was able to go on writing.

But write she did. The longest work included here, "Finish What You Started," was taken from a heterogeneous, small group of writings published posthumously and included in *Aftershocks*, where it really belongs. Its title is a loose rendering of the German proverb, "Whoever says A has to say B," meaning that, having gotten into a situation when it's cheap and easy, one has to continue when the going gets tough, to see it through. The story's vacationing narrator, having allowed her thoughts to drift off involuntarily and easily in a certain direction, is now goading herself to follow those thoughts through to their most likely unpleasant conclusion. The problem is that her tour guide at Chichén-Itzá reminds her of an SS trooper on guard at the rundown theater where Dutch Jews were assembled for deportation. Is he one and the same? Should she denounce him or shouldn't she? How will he answer her charges? In this tale, the reader senses a frantic search for justice as the mists of time and failing memory are blurring the horrible past into ambiguity and uncertainty. It is this story that will provide the greatest challenge to readers in their attempts to follow Weil into her own gray zone. The traveler, troubled by her personal memories, finds herself surrounded by the grisly remains of a culture laden with death and human sacrifice, now rearranged as a tourist site and profitably marketed as an intellectual – and in some ways even an aesthetic – experience. The question hovers in the fetid air: is it just the passage of time that makes the site she is visiting less vile than what she herself had experienced? Were the experiences those victims went through long ago as bad as what she carries in her mind? This story brings the reader to the vantage point from which Weil created her last novel *The Bride Price*, her literary counterpoint between Michal, the first wife of the biblical King David, and the modern Grete, at first hidden in an old house in the Netherlands, then finding her way back to life in a ruined Germany. It is a counterpoint that exists within the author herself, as well, between her subjective thoughts and feelings and her considered final judgment on humankind. On the one hand, she says that she "has Auschwitz the way some people have cancer," and that it will torment her to the grave; but on the other hand, she asks for justice toward past victims (single and collective) of man's inhumanity by reinvesting the bleached bones of the Old Testament story with the living flesh that suffered from ambition, murder, war, and attempts at genocide so long ago. She does not try to relativize the Holocaust, but simply and bravely, while personally suffering its afterpains, she points out that the past contained similar sufferings now covered over by time and conveyed by writings devoid of the gruesome details, and she questions whether mankind has progressed at all: A profoundly depressing thought, that, but fortunately and meaningfully it is opposed by the beauty of the novel's writing, its moral strength, and its conciliatory spirit. These are the balms that Grete Weil would have us use to soothe and perhaps cover the mark of Cain.

JOHN S. BARRETT

They who have gotten away with their lives are doomed.

Grete Weil
LAST TROLLEY FROM
BEETHOVENSTRAAT

Guernica

It was a while ago, back when Picasso's *Guernica* was still hanging in the Museum of Modern Art in New York. I'd made a date to meet Hans – or John, as he was called now – in front of the picture. We'd been friends when we were young, but hadn't seen each other since he emigrated. He didn't approve of the fact that I'd left Holland, the country where I'd found refuge, and had gone back to Germany, something which he'd let me know in one of his rare letters. I'd never pursued that – what was there for me to say to him other than "It has nothing to do with you, mind your own business"? Afterwards, we'd almost lost contact. Now, in New York, I'd called him up. He, who'd once studied history, art history, and philosophy – subjects with which he felt at home – had become a lawyer in the U.S. and headed, as he told me, a successful New York law firm, had married a Jewish girl from California, and had two children, a son and a daughter.

I'd suggested the *Guernica* Room as a meeting place. To my amazement, he agreed somewhat hesitantly, as if he didn't know where the picture was.

At the time we'd agreed upon, I'm standing in front of the Picasso, which I'd looked at two days earlier. And as was the case the day before yesterday, it's the horse more than anything else, the whinnying horse, rearing up in its death agony, that reaches out to me, moves me.

3

After a while I look around, because I don't want Hans to sneak up on me from behind. He's late. He never was one for being on time. I'm not sure I'll recognize him after all those years.

When he really does show up, I recognize him right away and he recognizes me, too. He's carefully dressed: dark pinstripe suit, gray tie, and a Homburg; his umbrella – as I found out later – had been left in the checkroom. He's trying to look like one of those Londoners from the City, but he looks very Jewish, just as he always has, and very German as well. He comes over to me with his swinging gait – even that's something he always had – holds out both hands to me and kisses me on the forehead.

Suddenly I remember that we – it must have been 1932 – had traveled together from Frankfurt to Maria Laach, where he gave an excellent, comprehensive lecture about the German Romantic movement.

On our way back, we'd stood on the station platform and talked about whether Hitler would come to power or not.

"Oh, come on! Never!" Hans had said. "It's all over already." At that moment it really was possible to believe that the Nazis had lost the approval of the voters. "But if it comes to that, contrary to every expectation, if he really does win the election, there'll be nothing for the likes of us but to get as far away as possible as quickly as possible. And no, I'm not afraid of doing that; after all, there's art in every country and there's nothing else I need."

After he lets go of me, we stand quietly in front of *Guernica* for a while, until he asks me in English, "Do you think it's beautiful?" Irritated by the question and because he's speaking English as well, I answer in German, "Of course it's not beautiful. But true. An outcry against war. And I certainly have a lot of sympathy with that."

He shrugs his shoulders and takes my handbag from me, at which I protest mildly and ineffectually. He goes on carrying it, something that men in this country often do, it seems, and leads me on through the other rooms. Stops in front of this or that painting and goes on talking to me in English.

Calls far too many of the pictures *terrible* and *awful* and says that he likes only very few of them.

I'm annoyed that I can't figure out what he likes and what he doesn't. In both groups there are abstract and non-abstract pictures: a Kandinsky that he likes and another very similar – to my eyes anyway – Kandinsky that he rejects. His whole way of looking at them comes purely from his feelings and seems somewhat chaotic. Earlier, I could depend on his judgment completely. He was a real connoisseur.

Because he persists in speaking English, I answer in my limited English as well, until I finally have to say, "I think you speak German better than I do English." He shakes his head vigorously. "I'm not about to speak German here in public."

Well, okay, there's nothing I can do about that other than smile at his fear of being mistaken for a German.

"It's a funny thing with you women. When my mother came over here after the war, she always wanted to speak German with me, which of course I wouldn't do."

I'm dumbfounded. "You spoke English to your elderly mother?"

"Of course. She wanted to stay here, so she had to learn it."

"Your mother had to go into hiding in an occupied country, lost her daughter in Auschwitz, and barely survived herself. And she had to tell all that to you, her only surviving child, in English?"

"Yes, of course."

This meeting is making me more and more uncomfortable. After we've looked at the pieces of sculpture out in the garden, where his attitude was the same as it was toward the pictures, he says we should have lunch at a little restaurant nearby.

We have to wait because all the tables are occupied, and sit a bit forlornly next to the cashier in the lobby. After a while, a girl in a black dress with a little, pink apron comes over and says in German, "You can come in now, your table is ready."

Turning pale, he points to me and says, "*The lady speaks English.*"

He pronounces lady as "laidy," just like that hill farmer in the Ticino who owned the chicken that one of my dogs bit the head off and who, like many Ticinese, had been in the States for a while and rightly presumed that we – a friend and I – would be more likely to understand his demand for an outrageous amount of money for his best Leghorn if he spoke English rather than Italian.

Only now does it strike me that Hans has a terrible accent and I really feel sorry for him.

The girl says forcefully, "But you're German."

He hisses, "And you're insolent," and follows her reluctantly to the empty table.

As we're digging into our shrimp cocktails, he says, "It's good, isn't it?" angling for a compliment.

I nod, long since used to the fact that everyone in America thinks that we never get anything really good in Europe. Then he asks me, without much interest, about my life during the last several years, about my plans.

I name a few of my book titles for him. The stories set in America he's already read, but immediately he says, reproachfully, "You're only interested in the blacks in this

6

country. I gave that up a long time ago. My interest is devoted to the Jews, understandably."

Even before I can reply to that, he goes on, totally unexpectedly, "I'd really be unhappy if my daughter Judy didn't marry a Jew."

But then I do contradict him. "So you think it's right for the unhappiness associated with being a minority to just go on and on?"

"I don't want my child to be treated condescendingly by an American family."

"What kind of people are you talking about anyway, John? I do hope, of course, that your daughter doesn't fall into the hands of Fascists. How old is she, anyway?"

"Fifteen."

"Then there's still lots of time." I'm really relieved.

There we are, sitting across from one another, strangers, almost hostile. And yet our youth was identical, we both grew up in cultured families, went to the university, and, because we were Jews, had to leave Germany before we could get around to doing what we really wanted to.

Turns out that he did it better, the right way, was more courageous than I was, went far away, to the U.S., put the ocean between himself and Hitler, got out of danger, found a new identity, built a new life for himself.

I force myself to think about what's happened to him despite all that. Because something has happened to him, that's clear to me. What is it? He didn't wait for the tread of hobnailed boots night after night, for the doorbell to ring, for the news the next morning about which one of his friends had been taken away during the night. He never had to send letters from a concentration camp and never received any from one.

Probably only learned after the war what Mauthausen

was or Auschwitz. Maybe hasn't even heard the names Sobibor or Treblinka till this very day. Was never expelled after the war, was never stateless, never a *displaced person* but as an American citizen possessed – as he and countless others thought – the best passport in the world.

He's never used ration cards (issued or forged) to get bread, he's never sat on the attic steps – the only place where he could be alone in the house of the people who were hiding him, on whom he was dependent, but who got on his nerves – writing down the things that moved him most deeply, from which he hoped to be able to give some shape to the future.

What's happened to him? Has his life just gone on too smoothly? Has that paralyzed him?

I look at him, say imploringly, "Hans."

"My name's John."

"Sorry. I forgot for the moment. But, actually, I just have to think about how much you've changed."

"Hopefully I have. A free citizen in a free country."

To keep the conversation from dropping off completely and because I know that, besides the arts, music meant a lot to him previously, I tell him that I once wrote the libretto for an opera.

"For which composer?"

"Hans Werner Henze."

"Don't know him."

Now I'm confused again. Earlier it would have been quite out of the question for him not to know someone like Henze.

"This Henze . . . a German?"

"Yes, of course."

"A Nazi." Not a question. A declaration.

"Not a Nazi."

"How do you know that?"

"He was born in 1926."

Obviously only half convinced he shrugs his shoulders and says, "To my ears modern music sounds like a bunch of cats screeching."

"Henze's music isn't all that modern."

"Was the opera performed?"

"Yes, often, even in the United States."

"What's it called?"

"*Boulevard Solitude*."

He smiles. "A little affected."

"Judged by today's standards, certainly. But the premiere was back in 1952."

"Where?"

"In Hannover."

"Did you go to it?"

I nod and again he shrugs his shoulders. "*Chacun à son goût.* Honestly, I don't understand you. The way you go running around that country. The fact is that the Germans killed your husband. Have you forgotten that?"

"John," I say, pleadingly. I'd like to get up, run away, just get away. But he says peremptorily, "We should pay a visit to my home. We'll get a taxi as soon as I've paid."

Not entirely what I wanted, but probably better than staying here. And it's a pleasant thought that he's going to get a taxi and not drive himself. I used to drive with him a lot, in his little Opel, and it was torture every time because he looked everywhere but at the road.

"Home" – an apartment decorated in good, middle-class taste, looking like everything had just arrived from the furniture store. No art anywhere. Nothing lying around, not a book, not a newspaper. The lady of the house, obviously just back from the hairdresser, looking very sporty and chic,

9

gives me a cool greeting – not very enthusiastic, but nothing to suggest that I'm intruding, either.

"My husband says you live in Switzerland."

"No, in Germany."

"Oh!" A frightened, anxious sound, as if a viper had slithered out of my handbag.

Their daughter, shapely, perfumed, wearing makeup – I would have taken her for eighteen – is sitting in a large easy chair in front of the television, which she quickly turns off without getting up.

John tries to explain things away and says to his wife, "But she has a house in Switzerland." He doesn't even blush at his lie.

His wife says, "We really love Switzerland, don't we, John? We've been to Zermatt and Engadin. Where's your house?"

"In Ticino."

"Don't know it."

John explains: "Ticino is sort of the Florida of Europe."

Then he asks his daughter – God only knows why – "Do you know who Picasso is?"

"Uh, some painter or other."

"He painted a famous picture called *Guernica*. It's hanging in the Museum of Modern Art."

"What does 'Guernica' mean?"

"Guernica's the name of a little town that was bombed by the Germans. A lot of children were killed."

"Jewish children?" She asks the question with a certain fervor, her big eyes – Hans' eyes – glow demandingly.

"No, the town is located in Spain. Spanish, Catholic children."

"Oh, yeah? Why are you telling me that, Daddy? It can't really be important to you."

"It's a world-famous painting. We could go to see it together sometime."

"You know I don't care a thing about paintings."

"Well, we won't if you don't want to."

The daughter of the man who once said that after all there was art in every country and he didn't need anything else. The daughter who wasn't supposed to marry a non-Jew has gotten out of her seat in the meantime and says grumpily, "You interrupted our TV program. I want to watch it some more."

"Whatever you like, *darling*."

Darling turns the TV on again and sits down in the big easy chair.

The rest of us are forced to stand there and watch. A war film is on. Viet Nam? Cambodia? I have no idea. In any case, young, attractive American heroes are fighting against the inhabitants of some jungle village. Oh, what do I mean, "fighting"? From an airplane, they're dropping bombs on a village made of straw huts.

The girl Judy sits there, bent far forward, with a ravenous expression on her face, but maybe I'm just imagining that. And with every explosion she makes a fist with her right hand and smacks it against the outstretched palm of her left hand.

I'm forced to watch, to see the bombs hitting and fire leaping out of the huts and suddenly I hear the horse from *Guernica* screaming in its death agony. I'd like to hold my ears shut even though I know it wouldn't do any good.

Hans looks over at me with an ashen, contorted face. Each time Judy smacks her hand, he jerks as if she'd hit him. Suddenly he says softly, in German, words clearly meant just for me, "There's no art any more."

., almost imploringly, "Come into my *study* with me."

ɪ glad to get up and follow him, then find myself fac-
nim in front of a gigantic desk in the big room that he
ɹls his *study* and in which there is not even a single object
that has anything to do with art.

Then he puts his head in his hands and I'm shocked to
see tears running down between his fingers.

Almost apologetically he says, "Judy can't forgive me for
getting away safely before the Holocaust. She can't imagine
how I could accept the murder of my sister."

"What does 'accept' mean? Were you supposed to kill
yourself?"

"Maybe I should have. My friends were tortured and
murdered in the camps, like your husband. But instead of
that, I went to the university here, to study law. There's nothing about me that she can hold on to."

After he's gotten all that out in a single breath, he repeats
tearfully, "There's no art any more."

"Of course there's still art, John. There's always been art
– as long as mankind has existed. Once you said – it was a
long time ago, on the way back from Maria Laach to Frankfurt – 'after all, there's art in every country and there's nothing else I need.'"

"What a memory you have. It's terrifying. Have to be
careful around you."

He wipes the tears from his face with his handkerchief.

I ought to leave now. What am I still doing here? And
he'd certainly be happy to get rid of a witness to his weakness. But curiosity forces me to stay and finally ask him.
"Tell me. How is it that you dislike so many pictures?"

"Me? What do you mean by that?"

"At the museum you told me most of the pictures were
awful."

"They are. Inferior and awful."

"*Guernica*?"

"Painted after '33 by the look of it."

"Picasso couldn't have painted it until he experienced the emotions caused by the bombing."

He glares at me. "As if such a picture has anything to do with reality. A nightmare. The fact is that with very few exceptions, nothing really good has been done since '33."

Slowly I'm beginning to understand. In '33 the curtain fell. The world ended then. His world. Mine, too.

But despite all, after a lot of bad times, I've found it again, even though it's changed. And now I also realize something else: the few pictures in the museum he *did* like were all painted before 1933.

He leans back and says again, as obstinately as a little boy whose toy train has been taken away from him, "There's no art anymore," and his look challenges me to agree with him.

But I counter by asking, "Do you agree with Adorno that it's barbaric even to write a poem after Auschwitz?"

"I don't know," he whispers.

"Look, John, I believe that art has much more to do with great sorrow than with great happiness, if there even is such a thing."

"They can't do anything anymore, the modernists," he says stubbornly and adds, by way of explanation, "Of course it's different for you than it is for me. I was a lover of the arts, you're an artist."

"You know, John, I don't particularly like that word. It's presumptuous and at the same time offensively modest. Singers are artists, so are musicians, painters, and sculptors. To be those things, you have to have learned something. Not everyone can. To be a writer all you need is some talent and a functioning brain. And a few powers of observation.

the word 'artist' has the disturbing connotation of
.ıe, of 'I can do what I want to, live however I want to,
vorld doesn't concern me a bit.' But what I do has noth-
g at all to do with that sort of feeling."

"More with politics?"

"Yes, John, more to do with politics. We, whom you
shouldn't call artists but writers or authors, we have the
accursed responsibility of telling people what's really going
on in the world and that human beings are murderers."

"Telling them about Guernica?"

"About Guernica and Auschwitz and a lot more."

"For example?"

"For example about dropping atomic bombs."

"Dropped by us."

"Not by you, John, and I hope without your approval.
But by your great big, free, democratic country."

"*God's own country.*"

"In order to accept that, it would be necessary to believe
in God."

"And you don't?"

"No, John, I don't. Never believed in God. If I had, I probably would have stopped after Auschwitz and Hiroshima."

He shakes his head sadly, moved by genuine sorrow.

"You'll die unconsoled."

"I'll die with the certainty that for me it's finally, finally
all over, that I'm entering the world of nothingness, where
there's no Hiroshima, no Auschwitz, and no Guernica."

"You hold it against me that I became a lawyer instead of
fighting?"

"No, John, the world doesn't need soldiers but laws and
people who know how to apply those laws. And besides, I'm
the daughter and sister of lawyers. There was no one whom
I loved more or felt closer to than my father and my brother."

14

"Why do you say that the world doesn't need soldiers?"

"Because I'm convinced of it, John."

"But one has to defend freedom."

"Who's 'one'?" What does 'has to' mean? And what is 'freedom'? Freedom for whom? Certainly not for the little people and the have-nots. For whom is 'one' doing the defending?"

My God, where have we ended up? He looks at me sadly. "You don't love life?"

"I have loved it very much, our green earth, and passionately, until people began to ruin it. What's left is sadness."

He shakes his head. "I love life very much. And my wife and my children, of course."

There it is again, that "of course," which I don't like.

But this time it helps me to finally get up and leave. He's gotten to his feet, too, takes my hand and shakes it firmly as he says, "It was a real pleasure to see you again. I don't know many people with whom I can talk about such things. These were two wonderful hours."

I nod; but that our reunion was a pleasure and that the hours with him were wonderful are things I just can't bring myself to say.

Without running into his wife and daughter again, I leave, flag down a taxi, and return to my hotel.

Don't Touch Me

No, Esther thinks, I shouldn't have come. My decision to never again set foot on German soil was dead right. So why'd I do it? Just to make my cousin Rosa happy? Never did care much for her. You'd think I didn't have it just great in New York. Why is it you always have to see something new? And now I'm sitting in a car next to this repulsive man who's Rosa's boyfriend. Why do you need a boyfriend at our age, anyway? And the guy doesn't even know how to drive a car, he's looking everywhere but at the road. And this goon is going on and on about the beauties of the Bavarian countryside. Awful, absolutely awful! Bavaria may be really beautiful, but not for me, not for someone who's been in Auschwitz. Rosa never lived through that. Rosa was able to hide out in Berlin. And stayed right there after the war. Well, if she thinks it's okay, be my guest. When was the last time I saw her, anyway? Beginning of the '50s, in Lugano. We were both there to take the cure at the spa, paid for by the compensation fund, to help me to recover from Auschwitz, her from hiding out. I don't think she was any more thrilled with me than I was with her. After that there was a parting of the ways. She moved to Munich, I went to New York.

And now she's tempted me over here with her pronouncements: "The Germans are nice and friendly." Grim and boring is what they are. And this guy who's driving me around. Always in the left lane. Now he wants to pass a truck. Are we gonna make it? Uh! We're past. There's a car to the right. Doesn't he see it? No! No!

Then a crash and everything goes black. In the middle of the night, Esther wakes up, has no idea where she is, feels around, touches cool metal, has a blinding headache, is nauseated. Is lying under a blanket, sticks one foot out. A hand takes it and puts it back. A few people to her right and left are talking back and forth, loudly, matter-of-factly. They're speaking German. She tries to lift her head – it doesn't work. Arms reach under her, she's lifted up along with the blanket; now she's lying on something that moves. Is being pushed into something that looks like a big tube. Then she screams out, "Not the gas! Not the gas!"

The young man in the white coat who's walking along beside her puts his hand on her arm and says in a friendly way, "What's wrong?" The nurse standing on her other side points to the blue, tattooed number on her arm.

The doctor goes on, softly, "Don't be afraid. No one's going to do anything to you. We just want to know what's wrong with you. To find out we need to do a CAT scan, a computer-assisted tomogram. Do you know what that is?"

She shakes her head. It hurts.

"You've been in a little automobile accident. Can you remember?"

"*No.*"

"You don't live here all the time?"

"*No.*"

"But you understand German?"

"*Yes.*"

"*Do you prefer to speak English?*"

"*Yes, yes!*"

He gives her arm a pat and immediately she starts to

scream again, but what comes out is more of a croak: "*Don't touch me!*"

"But I have to touch you. Otherwise we won't be able to find out what's wrong with you."

"*Don't touch me!*"

And it goes on that way. Whenever someone tries to touch her she screams. And it hurts to scream.

Rosa comes and says that the driver is all right, thank God. But he's in for a lot of trouble, because he was at fault. Esther could care less. Wouldn't care if he were dead. Serve him right.

The English-speaking doctor is there again and whispering something to Rosa – in German, naturally. Probably telling her that I'm a difficult case. Maybe he's right. Germany's a difficult case, too – for me.

So I'm dying, maybe. Done in by a German, fifty years later. Not bad at all. Makes some sense out of the whole business.

But I want to go back to New York, back to where I feel at home. Auschwitz isn't in Bavaria, but that fat Trudy who was always ready to hit us was a Bavarian. But she didn't grind me down in Auschwitz and she won't do it here, either. If she shows up, I'll have the law on her. Better watch out, I'm an American citizen. Can foreigners be treated without their consent? Here comes the doctor. He'll want to grab me again. *No, no, don't touch me!*

Esther gets her way for two days and one night. On the third day she dies of internal injuries that the doctors were unable to diagnose and is buried in Munich.

The House in the Desert

I hailed a taxi on Wilshire and gave the address. The driver, a white man, shook his head and drove on. There was a black man at the wheel of the next free cab. He said, "*Sorry lady*," before he roared away.

There was nothing left for me, then, but to walk up Wilshire. Up or down, however you want to look at it – the house numbers were getting lower, but since I was heading toward the hills, I had the impression that the street was getting higher. Up and down, *hinauf und hinunter* – was I getting closer to "*down town*," or was I getting farther away? Is it even possible to say "downtown," in this monstrosity of a city, where there are so many "downtowns"? Beverly Hills has one and so do Hollywood, Santa Monica, Westwood, Glendale, Pasadena, The Valley, and actually even Los Angeles itself.

Except for me, no one was on foot. Despite the full sun, the hills were enveloped by haze; in a few hours it was going to be foggy.

I walked and walked and walked, up – or down – Wilshire, one of the longest streets in the world. The longest is Sunset, which runs in a concentric circle. If I were out for a record, I'd have been better off going over to Sunset. An article in the *Los Angeles Times*, my picture on the front page, a new world record, "German Tourist Conquers Sunset Boulevard."

I'd started off in Beverly Hills, now I'd reached Holly-wood, so I left Wilshire and walked along Hollywood Boulevard, where things were less prosperous but there was more going on. The movie theaters were like booths at a carnival, slapped together quickly out of wood and papier mâché – exotic temples, Audrey Hepburn and O'Toole the size of houses, sidewalk plaques with the names of stars, some well known, some forgotten, and some you hardly know whether you've heard of or not. And that constant feeling of pressure in my head; the highly-touted California climate was not sitting well with me.

My feet hurt, I was hungry and thirsty. I had a cup of coffee in a drugstore and when I came out, the fog was there. Not black or yellow, as it is in London; gray strands wrapped themselves around my head, neck, and legs until, eventually, I was completely encased in thick cotton wadding.

The travel brochures, in which the City of Angels is a sea of white houses under a cloudless sky, don't mention the smog. The natives had told me that it had only been a problem the last few years, just since there were so many cars and factories. "What can you do about it, everything has its price." It was the prosperity-smog of six million people, the price people paid for one house after another, gardeners put up with it in return for their camelias and hibiscus, it was what actors had to shell out to buy the reputation of having been filmed in Hollywood, and immigrants used to the harsh climate of Germany didn't feel like they'd been taken advantage of when they had to put up with it in return for freedom and perpetual springtime.

I'd only wanted to stay a few weeks and didn't feel like paying anything but the bare minimum for such a short period of time. The fog was bothering me, filling my lungs, and making walking even harder. Silently, lights were gliding by. The United States is a quiet country. I pulled the wadding apart with my hands. It was tenacious. Sweat stood out on my forehead. I would have liked to turn back or sit down on a doorstep, or, if there were no doorsteps, on the sidewalk. Get a little rest and not think about anything and then maybe I'd be able to think about all the things that this awful climate had been sucking out of my brain for days. But I couldn't stop, had to keep on going, my uncle and aunt were expecting me, a reunion after thirty years, and they were old and fussy – almost certainly they'd made elaborate, expensive preparations for my visit.

Not that I could say that they were my favorite relatives. We'd always been pretty much strangers, never had much to say to each other, just lived in two different worlds. For a few years I hadn't even spoken with my uncle because he claimed that all Communists ought to be put up against the wall. The Hitler years, emigration, and persecution had softened my feelings; I felt sorry for these formerly well-off people who had to work at menial jobs to survive, he as an assistant in a law office, she as a cook, until they received a compensation payment. So I went on plodding through the fog and convinced myself that they'd really be glad for my visit.

Don't give up, keep on walking, through billows of poison gas, alone, vulnerable, at this end of the world, which is the exact opposite of that of our past. My uncle and aunt had managed – Poland was already beaten, the *playground* for genocide in German hands – to save themselves at the very last minute; long since given up by those of us who were living in Europe but outside Germany, they suddenly wrote from Cuba, where they were waiting to immigrate to the States.

How they, impractical and unrealistic as they were, had accomplished what the rest of us were unable to, remained a mystery to us and it was not likely that I was going to learn about it now. My aunt was always one for keeping secrets; every event, or whatever she considered to be an event, was immediately concealed from the eyes of the rest of the world. Once, after she'd fainted standing in line at the post office, she tormented herself and us for months by asking whether strangers had gotten into her pocketbook, from which absolutely nothing was missing. Of course, anyone could have been allowed to see what was inside, my uncle and aunt lived a life that was boringly proper. Trained to keep quiet, they wouldn't talk even now about their one real accomplishment – how they managed to get out of Hitler's Germany when it was already at war.

After a year in Havana, their immigration number came up and they moved to Los Angeles. "Such a wonderful climate," they wrote in letters that came via Switzerland to those of us now living in an occupied country, "flowers all year long, helpful neighbors, a higher standard of living, *God's own country.*" The latter fact they announced in English and they loved to drop bits of their new language in with the old one. "Not homesick any more, *not a bit,* not the slightest desire to return, ever." Really, if you thought about it the right way, they ought to be grateful to Herr Whatshisname that he'd made it possible for them to see the world. And their letters ended: "God punish England." The thought that anyone could understand whom they meant by "Whatshisname" and "England" seems never to have crossed their minds. At any rate, we never had any trouble because of it; probably even the censor thought their remarks were just too ridiculous.

Then we heard nothing more from them for a long time, until the end of the war, and then hardly any of us were still living. My uncle and aunt sent packages, clumsily tied together, but we were grateful for anything. They wrote that now we should finally come to America. Hardly a word about those who were dead, perhaps from tact, in order not to cause us pain. Whenever it was impossible to avoid mentioning names because of matters concerning an inheritance or something similar, they always put the adjective "poor" in front. Poor Eugene. Poor Elizabeth. Otherwise their letters were hardly any different from the earlier ones. *God's own country,* lucky to be an American citizen, freedom.

But it wasn't just sympathy that drove me on through the fog, it was curiosity, too. What were they doing with their freedom? Why hadn't they ever written about the dead? Why hadn't they ever asked what we knew about the fates of poor Eugene and poor Elizabeth? And about those of poor Otto, poor Leopold, and poor Selma? Why did they kill the dead with their silence?

The street – and I wasn't even sure that it was still Hollywood Boulevard – began to rise steeply and all of a sudden I felt sand under my feet. Yielding sand, drifting sand; very soon my mouth and nose were full of its tiny grains and I was coughing.

Despite that I kept going. Obstinately, grimly, as if before me lay some important goal that I had to reach no matter what.

Then, suddenly, the fog was gone; it hadn't dissolved, hadn't thinned, it was as if I'd walked through a wall and out into the open, into air that was easy to breathe, that already had the cool of evening about it. In front of me lay a desert – treeless, sandy undulations the color of a Siamese cat.

I felt a little intoxicated, but I liked the feeling. I liked the desert, its Siamese cat color that seemed softer, more appealing than the yellow I knew from pictures of the Sahara.

Only a landscape, no directions for using it, no trace of

a human being. Now the Siamese cat began to glow. It produced colors in its belly, they squirted out of its fur: bright red fountains, falling down into shimmering purple, then forming salmon pink, brick red, tomato red puddles, violet and sienna and umber around the edges. Covered with silver netting. *The biggest, the greatest, the most wonderful* – I began to think in the superlatives of this country. Neither skyscrapers nor bridges, nor concert halls, nor hospitals, nor department stores, nor supermarkets, not even the improvised awfulness of the *Main Streets* or the thousand-year-old redwood trees had ever had such an effect.

Abruptly, as if someone had thrown a switch, the magic ended, the desert was once again the beige-gray Siamese cat and when even the beige disappeared, it was as gray as all cats are at night; and after a while there was no cat at all, just impenetrable darkness.

Somewhere in infinite space, close by or far away, in front or in back of me, a dog barked. When the barking turned into howling, I remembered hearing that there were jackals here, but had forgotten whether jackals were dangerous. Although I was inclined to believe they weren't, I was afraid in the way you're afraid of something when you're a child, without really knowing what it is. You'd like to sneak off somewhere, crawl into a dark cave, have a wall you can touch, hear a comforting voice or one that scolds you, any voice will do...

Then I noticed the light. The small, flickering glow of a candle. I was immediately comforted, as if it were certain that the hand that had lighted it would protect me from the jackals. My confidence was curious. I didn't understand it. Since when had I trusted people? Since when had I not trusted them? Since I'd realized that they were murderers, or even before that?

The light – where was it coming from? From a farmhouse, a chicken coop. I doubted that there were farmhouses here. Chicken coops seemed more likely. Unlimited possibilities for running around, scratching; how the sand must go flying up in the air! Where else in the world were chickens permitted to find such fulfillment in scratching?

But it could be the hut of some blacks, too. If I were a black person and lived in this country, I'd rather live in the desert than in a city. Even with the risk that my chances of getting away would be very small if things really got bad. That much I knew, I knew about running away and hiding, that I'd learned – five years were long enough to become an expert.

Only five years? As if you could simply put aside a habit that had gotten into your very fiber. Once a body's picked up momentum, it doesn't just stop suddenly. It doesn't matter that there are no more Gestapo agents asking for your papers, that no trucks are driving through the streets to pick up people, that no one's ringing your doorbell at night, that the concentration camps have been turned into museums where cut-off hair and knocked-out teeth are displayed in glass cases, that there's no reason to run away any more. The running away goes on. Running away from the name. When Auschwitz wasn't yet a name, you didn't need to run away, but who's going to take the name back? Who's going to tell me it's not my hair, my teeth. They meant it for me.

Having to run away too late or too early – it'll never get that bad, my friends tell me, that's unthinkable in God's own world. When they drive me around their cities and we go through poor streets where no Whites live, they speed up and I know they'd like to cover my eyes. They tell me that lots of things have gotten better already, but it's not possible to solve the race problem from one day to the next. They shrug their shoulders, those tolerant and progressive friends of mine who'd probably be in danger down south because they were *nigger lovers* and who say, "You have to start from below, during the first years in school. Slowly, very slowly." And push the problem away from themselves and onto their children.

By now I'd gotten so close to the candle that I could smell it; it smelled like the hairspray I'd bought here, like *Desert Flowers*. I remembered the countless stores where nothing was sold but candles – big ones, little ones, colored ones, white ones, black ones, some for churches, some for the home, decorated with pictures and perfumed. *Candle light.* The very essence of the grand world, with a hint of dissipation.

My desert candle was a long, white spiral, held by a silver candlestick that was standing on a table covered by a white damask cloth, with silver place settings and Dresden china. It all looked very formal, un-American, and old-fashioned. Candlesticks of that sort were used at my parents' house when guests were coming whom we children called "of the highest category." But now I saw that it wasn't just a similar candlestick, but the very same one, one of the pair from my parents' house. I'd once made a drawing of it and knew its twists and turns, leaves and rosettes, and the spot on its base where it was a little dented.

And there were the gilded living-room chairs from the apartment of my uncle and aunt on Franz-Josefstrasse in Munich, the sofa covered in lilac-colored repp, and the heavy oaken buffet, in the central section of which was a perspective view of the Piazza San Marco, with the church in the background and the campanile on the right, all inlaid in woods of various colors.

I felt my way to the left through the darkness, trying to

find the door and the bell, but there was nothing but air and sand. Only after I'd circled the spot illuminated by the candle and returned to the point where I'd started did I realize that furniture, just simply furniture, was standing there in the desert, without a room, without a house.

I had scarcely walked into the light, across the threshold that wasn't a threshold, when two bony hands grabbed me by my shoulders and a face was pressed against mine. I could feel bristly hairs around the mouth that kissed me; I was touched – as far as I could remember, my aunt had never kissed me before.

She pushed me away and looked me over with her watery blue eyes. "Completely unchanged, can you believe it, after all those years." Of course she was lying – I was changed; I would have been deeply disturbed if I'd still looked like I did at the time when I didn't know that name. My aunt had aged, too, a tall, gaunt apparition in a shabby, black dress, with snow-white hair twisted into a knot and white chin whiskers. But I returned the compliment and told her that she, too, still looked exactly as she had thirty years ago.

She laughed boisterously, as if I'd told a joke, and called out in a whiny, domineering voice that I recognized immediately, "Maxie, come on out, she's here!"

My uncle, who walked over to me with an elastic step, was wearing a brocade house-jacket and because at first sight he looked like a young man, I had the impression that he was off to a masquerade ball, perhaps to one of those affairs where, according to family legend, he'd chalked up his share of stunning successes in his earlier years. Only after he'd held out his hand did I notice the sunken face and the deep fissures around a mouth that had been pressed into an unfamiliar shape by his dentures. "Nice that you're here. Were you able to find us right away?"

33

"Just let her catch her breath," said my aunt. "And of course she's hungry, you can tell by looking at her. And you're keeping her from eating, going on like that."

My uncle and I sat down at the table. My aunt pointed to the candlestick and said, "A memento of your dear mother." Then she went out, from one outside to another outside. When she came back, she was carrying a tray on which there were three plates; on each plate lay a green lettuce leaf heaped with a grayish-pink substance decorated with a lemon slice, an olive, and one of those little, red, sweet-and-sour California crabapples with the stems attached, the ones that look like radishes.

"We're eating *à l'américaine* today," my uncle said. "In your honor. Sorry we're not in a position to show you the beauties of our country otherwise."

"She'll find a way to do it," said my aunt, "she's just so clever."

I had no idea why she thought I was so clever, whatever she might have understood by that. How did I get that reputation? Had I ever put one over on her, sweet-talked her out of something or one of her countless secrets? Or did it just make her feel good to be able to say here, where nothing counts but success, "I have a clever niece," thereby concealing the fact that she hadn't heard anything about real successes but leaving open the possibility that, thanks to that quality, I might eventually have one.

The grayish-pink substance tasted awful, too highly salted.

"Excellent," my uncle said.

"Wonderful," said my aunt, "but don't think he's really happy with it. He always wants dumplings to eat."

"Or macaroni," said my uncle.

"Or apple strudel."

"Or *Kaiserschmarrn* with blackberry jam," said my uncle.

"Or veal shanks."

"Or weisswursts," said my uncle.

"Or liver dumpling soup."

"Liver dumpling soup!" he repeated, rolling his eyes. "Dumplings, *schöner Götterfunke*," he sang out. Suddenly he banged his fist on the table and yelled, "But I never get them! Never get them! Never!"

He swallowed the wrong way and started to cough. She jumped up and slapped him on the back. "Deep breaths, Maxie, take deep breaths! One, two, three, one, two, three."

"My drops," he gasped.

"One, two, three. One, two, three."

"Drops!"

"One, two, three."

She felt for the drops on the buffet with her right hand while continuing to slap my uncle on the back with her left; she looked like a big, clumsy raven that had broken a wing and was trying vainly to fly. Somehow she managed to give my uncle the little bottle; he took the stopper out and let the drops fall into a spoon.

"One, two, three. Deep breaths, Maxie. One, two, three."

"Dammit anyway, I think I've lost count. You with your damned one, two, three. Now I don't know whether there are ten drops there or eleven."

"Throw them away, Maxie. Quick!"

"No, I'm gonna take them."

"Ten drops is what the doctor said. Exactly ten. Throw them away Maxie, throw them away!"

"I'm gonna take them."

"Do you see the way he is?" she said and started to cry. "He wants to poison himself just to get back at me."

"I'm gonna take them, I'm gonna take them," he yelled

triumphantly and puffed out his sunken cheeks as she threw herself at him with a scream and knocked the spoon out of his hand.

"Thank God," she said and reached for a new spoon. "Thank God." Then she took the bottle and counted out loud. When she'd gotten to ten, my uncle said, "You left out seven."

"Are you sure?"

"Absolutely."

Carefully she carried the spoon out and brought it back washed. Then she started to count again. "Now there are ten."

"Yes," my uncle said, "now there are ten. But now I don't need them any more. My cough's gone."

We went on eating. After the grayish-pink stuff, there was fruit salad from the can.

"You have it good," said my aunt, "you don't need to cook for yourself."

"Sure I do. I cook for myself."

"No, over there everyone has a cook. And a maid. But no refrigerator. You have a cook instead."

"But I have a refrigerator."

"Ridiculous. You can't put one over on me. I know how people live over there. But your eyes must be popping out here. You didn't imagine *God's own country* would be like this?"

"Did you?" asked my uncle.

"Of course she didn't," said my aunt. "Don't you remember how overwhelmed we were in the beginning?"

"And we are still," said my uncle. "But now it's a different feeling. Back then we were *greenhorns*. Today we belong."

"We are Americans," said my aunt.

"Americans."

"Citizens."

"Of this free country."

"Here you don't even need to register with the police."

"That's freedom."

"You can do whatever you want to."

"Live wherever you want to," said my uncle.

"Then why are you living here in particular?"

"Los Angeles is the most beautiful city in the world," said my aunt.

"I don't mean Los Angeles. Why are you living all the way out here?"

"It's not way out," said my aunt. "It only seems that way to you. Our city is bigger than you Europeans can imagine."

"Well, okay. Maybe the desert climate is good for uncle's cough."

"Your uncle doesn't have a cough," said my aunt.

"Not a trace of a cough."

Since we were done eating, we sat down in the living-room corner, my uncle and I on the lilac sofa, my aunt on one of the gilded chairs. The night air was cool; I shivered.

"Can I please have a jacket?"

"No," said my aunt, whose neck was covered with goose bumps, "you don't need a jacket. It's warm here."

"Eternal springtime," said my uncle. "California has the best climate in the world."

"When I think of the way we used to freeze," said my aunt. "What we used to pay for heating. No power in the world would ever get us to go back there."

"Are things hard for you?" asked my uncle.

"She is so brave," said my aunt.

"Does he bother you a lot?" asked my uncle.

"Does who bother me?"

He bent over close to me, put his hand over his mouth, and whispered, "You know who."

"He's not there any more."

"They're all you-know-whats over there," said my aunt.

"But no one wants to admit it," said my uncle.

"Poor Elizabeth," said my aunt.

"Poor Eugene."

"You do know," said my aunt.

"I'm freezing," yelled my uncle. "Bring me my shawl."

My aunt jumped up; the gilded chair fell over. "My Maxie's freezing," she screamed, beside herself. "Quick, quick, we'll get Maxie a shawl."

She ran out, came back with a shawl and a blanket, which she wrapped around my uncle.

"Do you have a fever, Maxie?" she asked.

"No," said my uncle.

"Stick your tongue out."

My uncle popped his mouth open, stuck out his tongue and said, "Aaah." She waved the candle around in front of his face. "A little red, but not coated, thank God."

She sat down again. The conversation could go on.

"What were you going to say about poor Elizabeth?"

"Maybe I do have a fever," said my uncle, "I feel sort of funny."

My aunt stormed out again and brought a thermometer which she shoved under my uncle's tongue.

"Poor Elizabeth . . ."

"Be quiet," said my aunt, "that's much too sad. You can't begin to imagine all that went on there."

"Yes, I can, Auntie. They murdered her in Auschwitz."

The name hovered in the room without walls, filled it, trickled out into the desert, an explosive that I'd dragged

38

along with me from the other end of the world, in order to set it off here.

The effect was immediate; my uncle began to cough, the thermometer fell out of his mouth, my aunt slapped him on the back and screamed, "Shut up, shut up right now, you nasty person. Just look what you've done!"

"We don't want to talk about that," said my uncle and stopped coughing. "That word doesn't even cross our lips."

"We're not as heartless as you are," said my aunt as she picked up the thermometer. "Everyone wonders how you can live there. How can a person manage to forget all that so quickly?"

"Those you-know-whats are bad," said my uncle.

"The Americans are good," said my aunt.

"Democrats."

"Nothing like that can happen here."

There was a pause. Then they both said, "We don't want to know anything about it."

The sentence was only an interruption in the pause, a solitary exclamation point after which there was nothing more. I didn't have the slightest idea what could follow it, nor, obviously, did my aunt and uncle. There was absolutely nothing. In a certain sense, I was rather proud: causing absolute nothingness is not all that simple and demands iron resolve.

I was already beginning to believe that I would never succeed in breaking through it – with their "nibble, nibble little mousie" they had tempted me into the witch's house of their unwillingness to imagine, in order to stuff me with their obstinate not-wanting-to-know until I was as lazy and indolent and unsuspecting as they were, ready to be eaten – when suddenly everything began to change, dissolve into light and shadow, mild, uniform light and deep, bizarre darkness. Heavy became light, the table appeared to be floating, the sofa on which we were sitting, my aunt's chair, her hair – all took on the silver gleam of the domes of Saint Mark's. The featureless had taken on features, a desert style born of moonlight.

The moon hadn't risen, it was suddenly standing right over us, not the friendly moon from home, but a gleaming, open bowl. A foreign moon, hanging strangely in a foreign place. For the first time, I realized how far away from Europe I was.

My uncle had put his head back and was looking upward. Then he said softly, in a somewhat tremulous voice, "Once again your silent splendor fills field and forest."

He didn't realize he'd quoted it incorrectly and probably didn't know how the rest of it went, but for several moments it was obvious that the words had made him happy.

"Rubbish!" said my aunt, "there's no field or forest here. Don't get yourself excited over such nonsense, Maxie."

"It's by Goethe," said my uncle. "I still know that much. I learned it in school. That was a wonderful time. *Omnia Gallia est divisa in partes tres.*"

"He's educated, your uncle," said my aunt.

"If you're educated, you know the world," said my uncle.

"We went to Venice for our honeymoon," said my aunt. And pointed to the sideboard. "That's Venice."

"Saint Mark's Square," said my uncle. "There's a Saint Peter's Square, but I don't know where that is any more."

"You can't know everything," said my aunt. "We know Venice, Cuba, and America."

"And *there*," said my uncle.

"There, of course. But you don't have to mention that, that's where we're from."

"But I want to mention *there*," said my uncle, "otherwise she'll get an entirely wrong idea."

"There are mountains there," said my aunt.

"And our beautiful alpine lakes."

"And meadows full of primroses."

"And gentians, short ones and tall ones," said my uncle. "And Mischko the coachman who drives us to Bad Kreuth in the two-horse carriage."

"And the snow," said my uncle. "Especially the snow. The snow squeaks under your feet. The snow sparkles. The snow is white and clean."

"There's no snow here," said my aunt. "Thank God there's no snow."

"A *glückliches* country where there's no snow," said my uncle.

"Happy," yelled my aunt, "not *glücklich*, happy."

"Ja, happy," said my uncle. "That's what we always say, we're happy here but not *glücklich*."

"Shush," interrupted my aunt. "That Joseph woman is always saying that and I've told you a hundred times we shouldn't have anything to do with her. She's from Deggendorf and her father was a cattle trader."

"In general we only associate with people from Munich," said my uncle.

"Our beautiful capital," said my aunt.

"It has a royal residence and a court theater."

"And the royal gardens and the Oktoberfest."

"The Oktoberfest," screamed my uncle. "What kinda fancy talk is that. It's called 'Out'na Meadows.'"

"Don't get excited, Maxie. Okay, okay, the meadows."

"And our national anthem," said my uncle. "*God be with you, land of the Bavarians.*"

41

"And all of that," said my aunt.

"But you-know-who, you-know-who," said my uncle and shook his head.

"Trouble is that you-know-who can't stand us," whispered my aunt.

"Who can stand anyone?" asked my uncle.

"You can't say that," said my aunt. "People like each other here."

"Everyone's friendly to everyone else," said my uncle. "Neighbors help each other, the rich help the poor, the white help. . . ."

He stopped talking, looked at me for support, and cleared his throat.

"Careful, Maxie," yelled my aunt, "remember your cough."

My uncle remembered his cough and said forcefully, "Things are a lot better, but the race problem cannot be solved over night."

"The blacks are lazy and dumb," said my aunt. "I had a black cleaning woman. You can't imagine what I had to put up with. What a stubborn so-and-so. She never understood what I said to her. She had no idea of proper English."

"A lot of people don't understand us," said my uncle.

"But she was the worst one," insisted my aunt. My uncle nodded.

"It would be better if they were sent back to Africa," said my aunt.

"America for the Americans!" yelled my uncle.

"We don't need any blacks or Mexicans or Catholics," screamed my aunt.

"America for the Americans," repeated my uncle.

My aunt marched over to the buffet and opened the middle drawer – the one below Saint Mark's Square – and took out a star-covered banner, waved it around a few times, stirring up a cloud of sand and dust, then put it around her shoulders.

My uncle unwrapped himself from the blanket, stood up, and saluted. "Our country," he said, "is the home of freedom and democracy. Here the demands of the Atlantic Charter have been fulfilled. There is no poverty and no fear."

"Don't get excited, Maxie," said my aunt. "Don't get sick on me."

"We don't have enough money to get sick," said my uncle. "Getting sick is something only the rich can afford."

"If you're not rich, you're just a number," said my aunt. "Just a number on a conveyor belt."

"Things were different over there," said my aunt. "There the patient wasn't just a number."

"There he was a human being," said my uncle.

"Elizabeth and Eugene were numbers when they got sent to the gas. And Otto and Leopold and Selma. Or maybe someone gave them a phenol injection in the heart, or shot them, or clubbed them to death."

"Be quiet, you heartless person!" hissed my aunt. "Do you have to keep on talking about it?"

"We don't want to know anything about it!" shrieked my aunt and uncle in unison.

"We don't want to think about it," said my aunt.

"Or be reminded of it," said my uncle.

"We're not you-know-whats anymore," said my aunt. "*We are Americans.*"

"We've built a new life for ourselves."

"In this country," said my uncle, "where there are automobiles, radios, televisions, incubators, refrigerators, iron lungs, artificial kidneys, heart-lung machines, washing machines, dishwashers, calculators, typewriters, dictating machines, chirping machines..."

"There's no such thing as chirping machines," said my aunt.

"There are so chirping machines!"

"There are no chirping machines."

"There are so chirping machines, there are, there's everything here.

"Not chirping machines."

"Oh yes!"

"No. No chirping machines."

"Do you see," said my uncle, "the way she makes my life a hell. There are so chirping machines."

"And I'm telling you no."

"There are."

"There aren't."

"Chirping machines!" screamed my uncle. "Chirp ... chirp ... chirp ..." He couldn't go on talking; he was shaken by a fit of coughing.

"Don't cough, Maxie, don't cough," begged my aunt.

He went, "Chirp ... chirp ..." and saliva ran out of his mouth.

"Don't talk, Maxie, deep breaths." She slapped him on the back, looked for his drops, hopped around him, a big, black bird.

"Deep breaths, Maxie, deep breaths. One, two, three. One, two, three."

Then I left, heading in the direction from which I'd come, my feet sinking into the sand. I walked and walked and heard the "one, two, three" growing fainter and fainter behind me.

Little Sonja Rosenkranz

Marthe Besson was sitting in her small apartment in Paris. In front of her was a small stool on which she could prop her legs. At that moment there was a glass of red wine standing on it, next to the remote control for the television that was already turned on. Marthe was waiting for a film about the Resistance in France. Not that she actually needed to see the film – the years in the Resistance during the war had been the most significant time of her life. She'd helped a lot of people to "disappear" – Jews, political fugitives, and just plain patriots. After the war, de Gaulle himself had pinned a medal on her and squeezed her hand for a long moment.

She was curious to see how outsiders would present the Resistance in their film. She was not one of those people who didn't want to hear anything more about the war years. She scoffed at that attitude and believed that in order to honor the dead and to prevent fascism and war in the future, one simply could not forget anything that had happened back then. But she couldn't disguise the fact that her usual high spirits had given way to frequent periods of agonizing weariness and a vague longing for the active life she'd led outside the "law."

The previously announced film was starting. The credits paraded past her eyes. The names of the actors, the names of the director, the camera man, the editor – none of whom she recognized – then at the very end, the words: *artistic and historic advisor – Blanche Molitier.*

A blow to the heart. Marthe Besson let out a soft cry, sat bolt upright in her chair, her fingers squeezing the arm rests. Completely flustered, Marthe was simply amazed to think that it had been possible for her to totally forget the name of Blanche Molitier. That any person could repress things, even she herself, was something that never crossed her mind. She'd been just an ordinary teacher of English and German, someone who was always ready to fight against injustice, violence, and inhumanity – not a psychologist.

But now, with that name on the television screen, everything came back: the rage, the pain, but the old energy as well, and the feeling that the truth had to be found out at any price.

During the film, which she was hardly aware of, Marthe's thoughts were completely absorbed by what had happened back then.

It had all started with her visit to Heinz and Gaby Rosenkranz. They were both from Berlin; they'd met each other in a small bookstore that still carried books by banned German authors. As they sat over their scanty, wartime meal, Marthe Besson had begged them, as she'd done so many times before, to save themselves, to finally go into hiding. And as always, they'd rejected the idea of becoming fugitives and thereby endangering others.

But then Heinz Rosenkranz said that there was something that she, their good friend, could do to help them. She knew about their niece, didn't she? Sonja Rosenkranz, his brother's only child. They would like to know that at least the child was safe if anything happened to them. It couldn't really be so hard to find a place for her, she was blond, quiet, and well-behaved, didn't look a bit Jewish, wouldn't be noticed. And no one would have to take Sonja in at their own expense – she could pay with the money that had been smuggled out of Germany.

He got up, took a thick, sealed envelope from the cupboard, and pushed it toward Marthe.

Shortly after that evening, a neighbor called Marthe and told her that the Rosenkranz couple had been taken from their apartment in the middle of the night and slated for deportation. Little Sonja Rosenkranz had escaped arrest because she'd spent the night in a room under the eaves.

Marthe was on her way immediately. She found Sonja dissolved in tears over the deportation of her aunt and uncle. Said her parents had stayed behind in Germany. She didn't know whether they were still in their apartment or even still alive. But now she felt all alone in the world.

Marthe thought that any man would go crazy over such a charming creature. "Don't you have a boyfriend?" Sonja shook her head. "I had one. He stayed there, probably got drafted right after graduation. Maybe he was killed long ago."

She started to cry harder. Marthe understood the girl only too well.

Sonja accompanied her to the door, at which point Marthe again noticed Sonja's slight limp, the result of polio, but that little defect made her strangely attractive.

Marthe promised to return soon, when she'd found a hiding place. But it was as if someone had put a curse on the whole business; no one wanted to take in a fugitive. Finally a friend from the Resistance mentioned that there was a young journalist, Blanche Molitier, who lived alone in a rather spacious apartment and was known to be a good patriot and an active one. He got in touch with a friend who knew Blanche Molitier well and who told her about Marthe.

Marthe went to see her immediately. Any moment there

might be a new *razzia*. Blanche Molitier may have been in her early twenties, was pretty and well-groomed. Of course she'd take the young girl in. When Marthe mentioned that she'd be remunerated, she rejected the idea with an abrupt wave. The apartment was bright and pretty; Marthe was quite satisfied. That very same day she described the hiding place to the little Rosenkranz girl in the best light. Sonja said, "I'd go anywhere, even into some damp hole. Even outside Paris. I like it in the country."

On the television, the film about the Resistance was still going on. Marthe hadn't watched it; she sat there bent over, holding her eyes shut with her hand. Even today, she still didn't know exactly what had happened back then. Only that she, Marthe Besson, had failed – that much she knew.

The next evening she'd taken the girl – no, child – to Blanche Molitier. Sonja had made a sort of curtsy in front of Blanche Molitier, who had put her arms around the girl and kissed her. After Marthe had handed the envelope with the money to the Molitier woman and asked her to keep it for Sonja, she'd left, feeling really good about it all, and then had heard nothing from either of them for a long time – too long.

That had been right after Stalingrad, in other words, in the middle of the war. A few months before the liberation, Marthe read in one of those little, illegal handbills that were all over the place by then, that the body of a young, German refugee girl had been fished out of the Seine. She was described as wearing a coat without a star, but the place where the star had once been sewn on could still be seen. Thanks to the faded identification papers in her coat pocket, the girl's name could be established: Sonja Rosenkranz. Nothing else was known. Not even whether she'd thrown

herself into the river or had been pushed. At first Marthe
acted as if she were paralyzed, waiting days for a phone call,
for some sign of life from Blanche Molitier. Why had Sonja
left her apartment and ended up in the Seine? And where
was the money?

Marthe had waited and waited, but there was no word
from Blanche Molitier. Then Marthe had gone to the apartment to which she'd once taken Sonja. The concierge said
that Madame Molitier had gone away weeks ago. Where?
She had no idea. No, she didn't know anything about a
young girl living with Madame.

The whole thing was rather puzzling. Marthe asked her
friend from the Resistance about Blanche Molitier. No, she
didn't belong to the Resistance, but wasn't one of the "comrades," either. And where had she gone off to? He couldn't
say.

For weeks, Marthe tried again and again. The Molitier
woman had simply vanished. Was she a murderer? A thief?
A traitor? No, of course not – if she'd betrayed Sonja, the
girl would have been deported to Auschwitz or some other
camp and murdered there. But why the Seine?

When Marthe had finally freed herself from her trance
in front of the television set, she called the station, got
Blanche Molitier's number and dialed it immediately. "This
is Marthe Besson speaking," she said to the woman who
answered with the name Molitier. "Perhaps you no longer
know who I am."

"Yes, I do," said the other woman in an unfriendly tone,
"I think so, anyway. What do you want?"

"I'd like to talk to you. When may I come to your apartment?"

"I'm sorry. I'm going to be very busy for the next several

months. I'm hard at work on a book and it's difficult for me
to have visitors. I'm not sure I know what there is for us to
discuss. We hardly know each other."

With that she hung up, plunging Marthe into mute
despair.

What should she do? Blanche Molitier had vanished
without a trace for years. And then the years of monotony
at school had displaced her memories of the war. But now
Marthe had to know what had happened back then. Immediately, right then and there, had to know at any price.

She called an old friend from the Resistance whom she
knew to be patient and helpful.

"Do you remember the young German Jewish girl Sonja
Rosenkranz who was pulled out of the Seine shortly before
the end of the war?"

"Let me think. Sonja Rosenkranz? No, not really. What
was the story with her?"

"That's just what I'd like to know. I took her to a hiding
place at Blanche Molitier's apartment myself. How did she
get away from there and end up in the Seine? That's what I'd
like to know."

"After so many years?"

"I have to know. Even if twice as much time had gone by,
I'd still want to know."

There was a long pause; then he said, "Stay away from
that. It'll only upset you. What good's going to come of it?"

"There's something else."

"Yeah? What's that?"

"Money. Sonja Rosenkranz had a fairly large amount of
money. I gave it to Blanche Molitier myself when I took
Sonja to her."

"You think the Molitier woman stole it?"

"Yes, that's what I think."

"Do you have any witnesses? Can you prove you gave her the money?"

"I can't prove it."

"Then it's your word against hers. Blanche Molitier is a pretty prominent woman. They'll believe her, not you. My advice once again, Marthe, as an old friend ... stay away from it. If you were ever going to shed light on the affair, you should have tried to back then."

It was clear that he wanted to end the conversation, but Marthe went on talking. "I did try to talk to Blanche Molitier back then. It was as if she'd disappeared from the face of the earth."

"And after the war?"

"The same thing. Then someone told me she'd gone to Spain with a man who was wanted as a collaborator. To Franco, to the fascists. You really don't need to know anything more about the woman."

There was no holding Marthe back. She ran and ran, without looking to the right or left, ran amok, at first without any idea where her frenzy was carrying her. Then to her friends – and she had a lot – whom she asked for help. But no one was willing to try to uncover a cold trail. Each of them said, "A sad story. But it's all so terribly long ago."

It was, in fact, terribly long ago.

At one point an older man, a respected radio commentator – not a friend, but a close acquaintance – told her seriously, "Give up this senseless business, Marthe. It's not helping anyone and it's ruining your life."

But Marthe couldn't give up. A dam within her had broken and now she was being inundated by a flood of memories.

Why hadn't she kept the girl with her? Impossible at the time, with her many connections to the Resistance.

The Gestapo could turn up at her apartment any day. Why hadn't she investigated Blanche Molitier more closely? She didn't really know anything about the woman. Why hadn't she, Marthe, said to Heinz Rosenkranz, "I can't take the responsibility for your niece. I'd like to help her, but bearing the responsibility is too much for me. I have to worry about too many people, I have to get ration cards and forged identity papers together and distributed." Well, she hadn't said it and had assumed full responsibility.

Marthe inquired whether they'd autopsied people who'd drowned in the Seine during the war. They hadn't. Was there a list of such people? No list. Little Sonja Rosenkranz was no longer little. She grew and grew in Marthe's mind, displaced every thought but one: that of Blanche Molitier.

She called Blanche Molitier. But at the number she knew, she only got an answering machine. She wrote letters to which she never got a reply. She waited for her in the vicinity of her apartment. But would she even recognize Madame Molitier again? She must have become a fairly old woman in the meantime.

Then chance came to her aid. She was looking for a television program she was interested in and stumbled onto an interview with Blanche Molitier. No, she didn't give the impression of being an old woman; she looked well-groomed, fashionably clothed, self-confident, and several years younger than her age.

On the following day, Marthe was waiting outside the newspaper offices. And in fact, Blanche Molitier came out. She had a long, springy gait and looked even younger than on television.

Marthe slowly pushed her way up to her. "Excuse me, Madame Molitier, may I speak to you for a moment?"

Blanche Molitier raised her head and looked at Marthe

in astonishment. "For a moment, yes. What do you want?"

"You know who I am?"

"I think so. Madame Besson."

Marthe nodded. "Why did you do it?"

"Do what? I don't quite understand."

"Allow Sonja Rosenkranz to leave or send her away."

Blanche gave a short, hard laugh. "You mean that little brat who snuck off one foggy night? Rather upsetting for me, as you can well imagine. She knew my address and anyone who would secretly leave her hiding place would also be capable of betraying her host to the Gestapo."

"But she didn't do that."

"Thank God, no, and despite all the sacrifices I had to make back then, I came through the war relatively unscathed."

"And Sonja's money? Where did that end up?"

"What do you mean by Sonja's money? If she had any, she would have taken it with her."

"She didn't have it. I gave it to you. In a thick envelope."

Blanche Molitier rubbed her hand across her eyes. "I can't really remember."

For the first time, Marthe noted with satisfaction that the other woman was becoming unsure of herself and that for a moment, really just a moment, she was afraid.

Had she really mistreated the girl? Abused her? How did Sonja get to the edge of the Seine and what had happened there? A leap into the water or a shove from an unknown man or woman?

She would probably never find out and nothing more could be gotten out of Blanche Molitier. Her statement that Sonja had run away could never be disproved and no one but Marthe knew anything about the money.

One day, one of the few friends who still visited Marthe

regularly said, "Don't spend so much time thinking about it, Marthe dear – after all, thanks to your efforts Sonja was saved from the concentration camp. Specifically, from being driven naked through what they called 'the pipeline' at Treblinka and into the gas chamber."

"You think the Seine was less bad?"

Somehow Marthe got the point. But it's not so easy to give up an *idée fixe*.

Treblinka, she knew, had been leveled. But there were other camps that were still standing. Would she be freed of her Sonja complex if she saw those camps?

She was willing to give it a try. When she'd still been a teacher, she'd occasionally written things for several small French provincial papers. Now she contacted their editors and offered them articles on the former German concentration camps.

A few were interested and even prepared to assume part of the travel costs. Blanche Molitier was suddenly no longer so important.

And so it came about that Marthe traveled from concentration camp to concentration camp, from Buchenwald to Neuengamme, from Dachau to Mauthausen, and, finally, even to Auschwitz. She looked at everything with the same horror that comes over every visitor and reported about it all without failing to mention each time that the concentration camp was surely the worst thing that had ever been inflicted on a human being. In the end, she believed it herself and, with all that, the slightly limping figure of little Sonja Rosenkranz paled more and more and finally found a resting place where she – as Marthe now clearly recognized – had always belonged: in the sad company of those countless, promising young people who had died before their time, interred in mass graves by Hitler and his minions.

The Most Beautiful Spot in the World

The sea is gray and calm. Low clouds stretch to the horizon. Not a hint of sunny, fresh morning, but then it's barely past six o'clock. A long time ago, they'd called the Mediterranean the most beautiful spot in the world, he and Bella, when they were in Positano, drunk with happiness, and went wandering along the coastal road toward Sorrento and Amalfi, always high above the sea with its gentle waves breaking against the shore, emerald green along the edges, black above moss-covered rocks, then turning that incredible color, its real color, that deep blue which was somewhat darker than the sky and somewhat lighter than a violet. The essence of beauty. On narrow goat paths, they climbed up Monte Sant' Angelo, from whose peak they had the sea on three sides. Endless, enticing one to plunge in and forget the whole world. How Bella loved the Mediterranean. "I'd like to die right here," she said, "of happiness."

Now Bella is dead and he, Ben, is sitting in his car alone, parked on the side of the road leading from Santa Margherita to Portofino. He looks down at the gray surface of the water, his hands grasping the steering wheel. It wasn't from happiness that Bella died. She was killed in one of the gas chambers at Sobibor. Together with Ineke, their child. But maybe not together, either, maybe Bella had no idea that their little daughter with the un-Jewish name was so close by, dying the same horrible death she was. Had Bella thought of him, her dearest? Does a person who's choking from the gas think of anything at all? Was she relieved that at least he was safe in England? Safe? He was a Royal Air Force pilot who dropped bombs on Germany. He could even have been shot down. He wasn't shot down. After every flight, a safe landing. During every flight, thoughts of Bella, his beautiful, his beloved, who was waiting for him somewhere far below in Holland.

Why had he agreed to escape to England with his old flying friends, without her and the child, in order to fight for the allies? "Do it for my sake," she'd said. She wasn't really in any danger. Only young men were at risk. None of them had any idea, back in 1941, that all Jews were threatened. A beautiful young woman and a ten-year-old child. A gentle blond child with the un-Jewish name of Ineke.

Why did he run away and leave Bella and the child behind? Just not possible to take them along in the small plane that took off for England one night with young men determined to fight. The flight was anything but safe. How easily the plane could have been spotted and shot down. "Go, do it for me," Bella had implored him and then that terrible word *Mauthausen* rose up between them like a wall. Mauthausen was the place the young men had been dragged off to, and from it came the notification of their deaths. So far, no women had gone to Mauthausen, not to mention children.

Then he'd left.

After the war he flew back to Holland on one of the first planes. His parents had survived in hiding.

And Bella and Ineke? Stricken silence. They, too, had gone into hiding, were betrayed and deported. One woman, one child.

He goes over the lists of those deported; no one has survived.

He travels to Sobibor, finds nothing but gray earth, mixed with ashes.

Sometime or other he returns to his old life again. A test pilot, but no enthusiasm for it. He meets Rosa, no longer young, not very pretty, a widow who survived in hiding in Amsterdam while her husband perished at Auschwitz. Makes love to her without feeling love. Now she's sleeping in a hotel across the way in Santa Margherita, will awaken thinking they're going to drive to Cinqueterre that morning to spend their summer vacation there. He knows it's not going to be that way.

He doesn't want to marry her – he's told her that. How could he? He's already married. She doesn't like that. She wants to have a child with him. A child, after Ineke? Not possible.

With his right hand he opens the glove compartment. It doesn't take any great resolve. He's thought it all out long ago, every last detail. He looks down at what was once the most beautiful spot in the world and no longer is. Then he closes his eyes, sees Bella in the bright blue bathrobe, his last gift to her, with her auburn-red hair billowing around her. His beautiful beloved. He puts the muzzle to his temple. His hand is completely calm. He smiles, then pulls the trigger.

Finish What You Started

The bus from Mérida to Chichén Itzá was fast but its springs were in sad shape. There was no one sitting beside me. In front of me, a nice-looking American couple, gray-haired, sporty. The rest of the passengers were Indians. Several got out along the way, but no others got on. A good way to travel despite the discomfort. I was happy that I hadn't let the young man at the Barbachano Travel Agency talk me into a taxi the previous evening. "Your chauffeur, Madame, will provide an informative trip through the archaeological sites." That sentence, which was supposed to entice me, elicited a "no."

It was hot and humid in the bus. I looked out the window at the flat countryside, at trees and bushes that gave the appearance of Dutch woods in the springtime, but in reality it was a jungle with vultures circling overhead.

They circled quietly and persistently, patient birds that can wait; what they need to live – death – is always around. There had to be a lot of death in the jungle; whenever I raised my head I saw swarms of vultures, dark, ominous above the bright green.

The woman in front of me turned around: "The vultures ruin every trip to Mexico for me." Without introduction, completely preoccupied with her problem. "They're just too horrible."

I like the noble, Roman word *vulture* better than the German *Geier*. Unlike the German word, it has no association with other words like *Pleitegeier* – slang for the threat of bankruptcy – or with the devil or Florian Geyer or the Geyer who may have been Richard Wagner's father, or with my math teacher, the nail-chewing Johannes Geyer. Naturally, I'd thought *Geier*, but now replied in English that I thought the vultures were beautiful.

"I don't understand that. What do you think is beautiful about them?"

"The peaceful way they fly."

"It's deceiving. They're looking for prey."

"Even vultures have to live."

"And those awful, naked bodies."

"But you can't see them at this distance."

"But you know what they look like. Revolting, absolutely revolting. And besides. . ."

She hesitated and blushed like a schoolgirl who's found a dirty passage in Ovid. Then she summoned up her courage: "They just remind me of death."

An even deeper blush, then a hasty turning away, nervous paging through a book about the Mayan country.

The bus roared on, ran over a dog; I got nauseated, but I'd taken something for motion sickness and the urge to throw up passed.

Short stops in poor villages, always the same straw-covered huts around a church in Spanish Colonial style. The inhabitants barefoot, men in trousers and shirts, women in long, white dresses with red or blue embroidery along the hems. Jugs, baskets, bundles of wash on their heads. Closed, Mongolian faces, many thousands of years old, measured movements, dignity from a distant time.

Shortly after one village there was a dog lying on the

road again – maybe running over dogs is a sport here – with vultures sitting on it, pecking away. Scared off by the noise of the motor, they flew away. The dog was still moving.

The woman turned around again. "Do you still think vultures are beautiful?"

"Yes."

This is a country one ought to ride through. Alone. Nobody asking you questions. Figure out for yourself what's beautiful and what's not. Forget immediately what you thought about. Don't open your notebook, throw your watch and compass into a pond. Burn the letters you got from home without reading them. Whistle something to yourself, polish up a few verses, tell yourself a story. Without a beginning or an end, without a climax, without anything sensational. On horseback.

The woman read her book; the chapter was about Chichén Itzá.

An educated, appealing American woman, able to be independent of her husband, traveling in an Indian bus and taking the trouble to read instead of letting herself be told by a travel guide where and when she should look and for how long. And doesn't want to know anything about death that's lying on the road.

Shortly before we arrive, she turns around again. "If you haven't reserved a hotel room, I'd recommend you try the Hacienda. You can stay there for half as much and it's a lot nicer."

Certainly a piece of good advice. I climb out of the bus behind her, handbag and camera in my left hand – even I'm carrying the equipment required of every tourist – and my little suitcase in my right hand. Stand there in the parking lot crammed with Barbachano's taxis and the pullman buses of travel agencies, ask an Indian for directions, walk on down the asphalt street, and after ten minutes reach the Hacienda, which, like the hotel, belongs to the unavoidable Señor Barbachano. But whether even his unerringly good business sense had failed to make something of this countrified inn, scarcely a kilometer away from all the hubbub, or whether he was cultivating an air of peacefulness here for eccentric loners, the pretty garden between the main building and the bungalows was deserted. I got a charming two-room cottage just for myself, showered, changed, and went back the same way I'd come.

In the roadside ditches, iguanas, their prehistoric heads peering curiously from the grass, then pulling back shyly when anything approached, so that only gray, armored backs and striped tails were to be seen. Vultures and iguanas, red bushes with clusters of long, blue flowers, trees smothered by still-closed orchids, aerial roots, yellow, red, blue, and orange butterflies, the fragrance of blossoms, and shimmering heat in February. No doubt about it, I was in a tropical country; yesterday, after landing in Mérida, I still hadn't really believed it, despite the warm wind.

The fulfillment of old longings, childhood dreams, to be somewhere where it's different, in a really foreign country, without – as was the case in Southern Italy and Greece – the feeling of having come home. That there were temple ruins here was something I looked upon as a bonus – I knew far too little about them to have come here just for that reason.

Past the hotel, above the treetops, a temple-crowned pyramid, then an entrance with a wooden barrier like those in front of soccer fields. At a table, admission tickets. "One please and a brochure about Chichén Itzá." A meadow where there'd once been a city, but now nothing more than ruins in a broad semicircle. I looked up their names on the diagram in the brochure. They were called El Castillo, Building of a Thousand Columns, The Warriors' Temple, The Platform of Venus, The Platform of Tigers and Eagles, Tzompantli, Jaguar Temple, and Arena of the Ball Games. Groups of tourists proceeded from one sightseeing attraction to another, flecks of color between green grass and gray stone. They walked, I stood, they stood, I walked. Over to the Warriors' Temple, which appeared to be the best preserved – magnificent, gloomy, threatening. More threatening the closer I came and the more distinct the details became. Art divorced from man; where humans did appear, they served a purpose, were warriors or sacrificial victims. Of the victims, all that was to be seen was the heart, the heart in eagles' talons, in tigers' claws.

"That is a snake," said an Indian guide close by and pointed to a stone monstrosity on the ground with wide-open jaws and chunky teeth, "and that's an eagle that's grasping a human heart." Eyes right, eyes left, eyes straight ahead. "Sit on the snake, a little bit farther back, honey ... now smile." "A little more to the left ... no, I mean to your right, otherwise your head covers the heart." The pictures were taken, the photographers' wives in their red dresses relaxed, the group marched off.

And I was alone again, with the snakes, the eagles, and the hearts, hearts cut and ripped out of breasts. Why was that done to them? Always the same, from the earliest beginnings, only the method changes. People never learn. And, of course, they always have an excuse for it, power always finds an excuse for every cruelty.

In the brochure it says, "The gods, the great workers who caused the corn to ripen, had to be nourished with human blood and human hearts."

Belief, superstition, is it more permissible, more excusable, less cruel if there's a religion behind it? Whitewash over

69

the demonic, frightful lust disguised as art, made suitable for travel groups by the patina of time. Wrapped up in tissue paper by Barbachano and offered to his esteemed guests.

Reluctantly, curiously, I walked through a dangerous, brutal, but sometimes even beautiful dream, through uncertainty and fear, powerful even after hundreds of years . . . until I came to a platform enclosed by a wall, which finally displayed something human other than butchered hearts. From the flattened corners, four rows of death's heads, one above the other, extended out to both sides. On the edges, full face; on the long, flat surfaces, full or quarter profile. Only the cornerstones still had their original white color, to the sides the top and bottom rows were blackened, while the two middle rows varied from pink to orange.

Mass death as ornament, like stylized skulls sketched for practice. Some artist had not reacted to death passionately, but coolly, as if it were a problem of form.

For a moment I hadn't been paying attention and now I was surrounded by an American travel group. "This is where the skulls of the sacrificed were kept," said the guide: "The platform is called Tzompantli, which, in Indian, means something like 'wall of skulls.'" He paused briefly before adding, "The Black Wall of the Toltecs."

A bored voice. My God, what do I want? The man has to rattle off his little speech day in, day out. Probably I'd expected more from him because he looks different from the other guides. Not Indian, certainly not a Spaniard, either; a gentleman with graying temples, more likely English than American, a retired officer right out of the book, I've seen him a hundred times already, on stage, in movies – a comic figure, broad shoulders, narrow hips, clipped moustache, pipe in the breast pocket of his tweed sports jacket.

He returned my stare with a supercilious look, then turned away, tossed me aside like something useless that had fallen into his hand by chance. I've had this experience once before, this wall, these tourists around me, that phrase, "The Black Wall of the Toltecs," his disdainful look. Nonsense, I've never been to Mexico, never even to this continent. But the man – I've seen him before. Quite certain. Probably. Maybe I'm just confusing him with someone else of his type.

A young blond woman drew something quickly in her sketchbook. "What are you doing that for?" asked an older man.

"What for? Not for anything. For myself. I find it interesting."

A cool, attractive person, elegant and self-confident, with a hysterical mouth.

The guide looked on in amusement, then put his hand on her shoulder and said, with seduction in his voice, "You're quite an artist."

They walked on; I stood in front of the wall, in front of four rows of death's heads, black, white, orange, pink, weathered by the sun, weathered by rain and wind, blizzards of Yucatán, tornados of Chichén Itzá, but their form has remained – men's skulls, women's skulls, no longer distinguishable, alike in death, Indians, blacks, Gypsies, Jews, always the same, throughout all time, timeless, their end a mass grave and we, intercontinental pleasure travelers, say "How interesting." Yes and amen.

New tourists came along. I walked away from the ruins on a broad path leading into the woods. After two or three hundred yards, a round pool far below, enclosed by almost vertical rock walls. Despite the steepness, flowering shrubs were growing between the rocks. A beautiful spot, short, fragrant grass, good for stretching out on when you're a little tired – just let yourself drop, like you're taking a rest during a mountain hike.

Two iguanas were playing on the rim of rock – child's play, love play, I don't know. It looks posed, but dangerous, too; might be a fight, man-to-man, hard, armored backs, but they can probably be wounded in the belly. And when it's over, the stronger turns the weaker one on its back.

The grass smells like it does in the Ticino. But are there snakes? Across, on the other side, the U.S. side of the Gulf of Mexico, it's well known that snake-filled swamps are good places to let lynching victims disappear. But there's no sign of a swamp here. Everything's dry. Too dry to be productive. The pool is the only source of moisture. Was it always here? Is it artificial?

The brochure. That's what I bought it for. A whole chapter entitled, "The Sacred Cenote." The spring, the well, the pool that made it possible for the Indians to settle there and provided the name Chichén Itzá – "the edge of the pool where the Itzá dwell." Sacred? Why sacred? What follows *sacred* is *sacrifice*. Above the iguanas, vultures circling, pool of sacrifice ... young girls and women thrown in before dawn. If one of them didn't drown by noontime, they pulled her out and worshiped her as a goddess. If you want to be worshiped, learn to swim, but remember that you're going into the water weighed down by jewelry, in long, tight-fitting garments, bikinis are still reserved for dancers, but a few years after Hiroshima everyone can have them, A-bombs on bikinis, sex-bombs in bikinis, bomb-conscious thinking: a bombing incident, the play bombed, an impact like a bomb, napalm bombs, fire bombs, A-bombs, H-bombs. Only when you're talking about the one that might be meant for you yourself, do you abstract it and express it in the singular. So it is with this pool that sparkles in the sun. Beautiful, endearing. Still waters run deep. What's down there is seldom seen again. What's gone is gone. Even your own past. Vain attempt to imagine yourself at the Auschwitz trials, that it was those very same shabby-looking old men. Can't get away from the impression of run-of-the mill actors performing a Grand Guignol play in some congenial local theater. Key words: phenol injection, selection, political section, Boger's swing, Lili Tofler, Block II, *schwarze Wand*.

Schwarze Wand, "black wall." The Black Wall of the Toltecs. The black wall of Auschwitz. Bored voice. Was that description something the Englishman thought up? What does the brochure say? The brochure says nothing. Not a word about the Black Wall. Maybe I'm translating it incorrectly, *Mauer, Wand, Wall,* they all mean "wall." *Schwarz, dunkel, finster, düster, abscheulich*: "black," "disgusting." How many combinations can you get out of three and five, why should mine be the only one that makes sense? The Black Wall of the Toltecs. The definite article and the designation of the tribe invite comparison. I'll accept the challenge. It's meant for me.

Not a breath of air stirs the water. The wall, in front of which murders were carried out, blood-darkened stone. Who's challenged me? An English-speaking tour guide? A minor employee? Is he really English?

I picked up a fist-sized rock and threw it into the water. Hit dead center. The circles in the round basin looked as if they'd always been there. My handiwork. For the eternity of the moment. If I close my eyes, I see that fellow. Hear him. The Black Wall of the Toltecs. How does it go in German? *Die schwarze Wand der Tolteken.* Entirely possible that it's a German voice. An actor who emigrated? No, no emigrant.

But theater. Wasn't I just thinking about the theater? About something that reminded me of the theater? On stage, the court and the murderers. The witnesses in the audience.

Witnesses in the audience, everyone a witness, the parquet of a suburban theater, the rows of seats taken out, the chairs and tables gone, the stage cleared and empty, people, a lot of them, knapsacks around their necks, rucksacks, in overcoats that are too big for them, that hang loosely, similar clothing, uniform faces, gray, resigned. Stale air, sweat, and disinfectant, the *Hollandsche Schouwburg*, the theater in Amsterdam, called the *Joodsche Schouwburg* in 1943, for the interval between arrest and deportation the improvised prison of the Central Administration for Jewish Emigration. Emigration is what they called it in front of us; among themselves they designated it the Final Solution, but that's probably prejudiced by what we know today – the *Scharführer* and *Unterscharführer* would hardly have known the word. The *Hauptsturmführer*, very likely. On my green portable Remington, I typed letters dictated by prisoners to friends or neighbors. Asking them for some article or other, or to look after the dog and the canary until they came back. Believed they'd come back. Not all, but most of them. "You think so, too, don't you Miss?" "Yes, I think so, too." Typed their nonsense and typed and typed. Night without end. But my shift goes by. I put the cover on the machine and slip the notes with their illegal requests into my brassière.

Dirty, tired, hoarse from all the talking, that stench in my clothing, my hair. Outside in the lobby, an SS man. "The student." No longer know whether we just called him that because he looked nicer and smarter than the others or because he was really a student. One of my co-workers claimed he read Stefan George and Rilke and knew something about archaeology.

"You can't leave now, the air-raid alarm's sounded." Just mentioned it casually, wouldn't matter a bit to him if I got my bicycle and pedaled home. Not one of the heel-clickers. I'm almost past him when he says, "Of all the women who work here, you have the most beautiful eyes." A warm bath for my filthy skin. I stop and turn around. He looks at me superciliously. Walks away, whistling.

A trip home in total darkness, the antiaircraft guns firing like crazy, searchlights probing the sky, the planes droning by at high altitude. My blue headlight is so weak that I'm sweating with exertion. But it doesn't matter, not today.

When did I realize that I had no reason to be pleased about the compliment? Not on the way home, maybe the following day, maybe a week later, sometime or other it was just there, the revulsion toward a person who was sending the likes of me to their deaths night after night and whistling while he did it and who would be whistling on the night when it was my turn. But not someone whom you could convince that Jews were vermin that had to be exterminated. Vermin don't have beautiful eyes.

The Black Wall of the Toltecs. You have the most beautiful eyes. Is it the same voice?

I never saw him again after the summer of 1943. Have no idea where he was during the last two years of the war. At the front? A guard at Auschwitz? That he's living here, probably under a name that's as phony as his getup, is evidence against him. But I can't prove anything. And if I could? Would I go to the German Consulate in Mérida – if there's one there – and demand his extradition? Or to the police? Or to Señor Barbachano and tell him to fire him? That might have some hope of success; Barbachano has to think about his Jewish customers.

He was standing there beside me, in the middle of his

group, pointing toward the pool with his pipe. "The Great Cenote, the sacred spring."

He says nothing about the sacrificial victims. No one asks; a young woman exclaims, "How lovely!" The blond is not looking at the water but at the man.

I'm looking at him from a lower angle. The little moustache is just a thin shadow, his mouth free, a sensual, arrogant mouth above a weak chin.

It's him, no doubt. I'd love to see his face if I went up to him and said, "*Guten Tag, Herr Weber.*" But is his name really Weber? It could be Wagner or Werner, or even Winkler. I've forgotten his name, all I know is that it starts with W.

"Ladies and gentlemen," he says, "I think we've done a good morning's work and now it's time to enjoy a well-earned lunch. Those who have brought theirs along can find a spot to relax in this romantic setting, the rest of us will go back to the hotel. In exactly two hours, we'll meet again at the entrance."

Two men who are carrying their lunch bags in addition to their wives' pocketbooks spread their coats on the grass for their ladies; the others follow W. along the broad pathway to the exit.

Tag along, so as not to lose sight of him. From behind, he looks thirty. But has to be forty-five, at least.

If it's him. Twenty-five years is a long time. A generation. After twenty-five years, can I recognize someone who was basically a stranger, about whom I know nothing beyond a few sentences? Why do I want to recognize him, anyway? He didn't do anything to me. He never whistled at me, I wasn't deported, I managed to get away.

Through the long, dark corridor that once connected the stage entrance with the dressing rooms. Without knowing whether someone was standing outside. If someone had been standing outside it would have meant Auschwitz or Treblinka or Sobibor. An even surer death than what the maidens faced at the sacred pool. No divine intervention in Eichmann's bureaucracy. No one was standing outside. W. stayed inside, although he knew, of course, that this was an escape route. Not because of my beautiful eyes. Probably just laziness. Last roundup of the last Jews. One last time – the last time even for the SS – a lot to do. It was a criminal offense if anyone got away, so there were a bunch of additional forms to be filled out. Besides, we were his Jews, just the way our chickens were my mother's chickens, so she didn't want to eat them.

After the stale, smelly air, outside in the clear morning. The star torn off my coat, starless again for the first time in two years, an ordinary person, someone walking through sleepy Amsterdam in the early morning, through the delicate September fog toward a hiding place, toward a vague, small freedom she believes – at least still did, then – will eventually turn into a great freedom.

Not knowing that this is the hour of the greatest freedom of all. Not doing what the law commands. Antigone buries Polynikes. The assertion of love against hate. I'm denying hate its sacrifice, not stretching out my neck. An option for life. When you think about it, W. helped me to it and I ought to be grateful to him for that.

The group had reached the road. W. out ahead with the blond, carrying her sketchbook; she'd lifted the Leica from around her neck and was stopping now and again to photograph something. The others followed suit and even I played photographer, held my camera chest high and saw W.'s arrogant face in the ground glass and the wild infatuation of the young woman.

Indians came toward us when we were almost at the

hotel, two men and a woman, not in the costume of Yucatán, but looking much more picturesque; their trousers and skirt, jackets and blouses were of brightly colored fabrics, mostly striped, in striking shades of red.

Absolutely made for a color slide. Doubtless staged by Barbachano. Street duty between 11:30 and 12:30 when the tourists are coming out of the temples, another hour later in the afternoon, and then a dance in the dining room in the evening. Are they on a salary or dependent on tips?

They turned away from the cameras and covered their faces with their hands. Directing's not bad, a little shyness jacks up the price.

"Please, please," said the blond and threw a coin toward the woman. It landed on the street. No one picked it up.

I was wrong. They didn't want to be photographed. Their discomfort was genuine.

A few Americans walked around the Indians with their cameras, encircling them.

"Please, please." Already less friendly, insistent, don't make such a fuss, we don't have much time, our lunch is getting cold.

W. watched. It would have been easy for him to have intervened, but he didn't, just held the sketchbook in firmly crossed arms and puckered his lips as if he were going to whistle.

Between splayed fingers, dark eyes looking for an opportunity to get away. There wasn't one.

"Don't make such a fuss," said the blond, "it's not going to hurt."

Maybe it does hurt, how do we know they're Christians, maybe they're not. In Guatemala I once saw two men burning incense and corn on top of a hill, praying with their arms stretched over their heads. Maybe it does hurt, maybe it is bad for the soul when an image is made. Draped mirrors, incantations, started out in the east, migrated further to the east, never got to where they were going.

Diana, the blond goddess from the U.S.A., lifted her weapon, let out a shriek, "just look here, it only takes a fraction of a second!" but that fraction of a second sufficed for the Indian woman to spit, and the slimy blob landed in the middle of the blond woman's face.

She screamed again, different now, shrill, ugly, no longer a goddess but a little girl, frightened to death. W. wiped the spit away with his handkerchief, but when she didn't stop crying, he put his arm around her shoulder and said, "Ah, it's just an Indian."

She understood immediately that he was giving her the opportunity to make victory out of defeat, nodded, wiped her nose, and attempted a shy smile.

But when he withdrew his arm, she produced a few more sobs, at which point he took her by the hand and pulled her along with him.

The others followed. They'd been rendered speechless.

Away, just get away from there. Eat at the Hacienda, lie on the bed, unable to sleep, then the decision not to return to the group, never to see W. again, never again. Forget him. A path in the woods, blooming cactus, hummingbirds, bigger birds, brilliant red, a really huge one with a long, golden tail. And always that fragrance. A place of enchantment, but I'm not one who can be enchanted, not any more, not today, not tomorrow, not in Chichén Itzá. It would have been better to stay at home.

To cry at home, without going to all this fuss, in your own bed, on the mattress into which the shape of your body has been pressed, where lying down is less difficult than in any other bed, and sleeplessness is a sort of hovering between finally-knowing-how-it-really-is and dreaming, not a punishment made worse by the smell of insect repellant, disinfectants, and poorly dried underwear, by thirst because *eau non potable* is printed above the faucet which drips all the time to boot, or by the snoring or groans of love-making from the adjacent room. To go walking in the park in front of your house, feeling your way from tree to tree with your eyes, each tree a support proven dependable by this time, accompanied by your dog. To get some coldcuts for supper at Engelhart's grocery on the corner and say, "Oh, this bad weather," or "the warm sun," and Herr Englehart answers whatever's fitting, "Yes, yes, the atom bombs" or "The world would be really good if people behaved as they should," and if the store isn't full he'll whisper something more, he knows for sure that the Yanks have a secret pact with the Russians and "we're the ones who are always the dummies." That's what he says but doesn't mean it, because, of course, we're the cleverest ones – clever, innocent little lambs who are sometimes just taken in by a wolf in sheep's clothing. Engelhart, one of those deceived, the fellow traveler, the opportunist, you know where you stand with him, know his failings and his good qualities, and are under no illusion that he wouldn't be ready, anytime, to toss you to the first wolf that came along looking for a meal.

But why travel when traveling is a torment, why give in to the desire to let yourself be bowled over by the beauties of the world as you did back then, when the world was still beautiful, why risk meeting the W.'s, who, at home, are indistinguishable from the Engelhardts in a setting of well-stocked butcher shops, comfortable pubs, and the new German friendliness in municipal offices, men who've hung up their pasts on the handiest nail while you're vainly searching for your own? Why travel from one sightseeing destination to another, reading in your Baedeker about who got killed where, when, why, and how, and thinking – like the "how lovely" exclaimers – "that was all so long ago"? When does the past start? When the blade falls or when the corpse is consigned to a mass grave or burned in a crematorium or when the murderer dies or when there's no one left alive who loved the murdered one or when the first tourists buy their tickets to the execution site? Do the latomias at Syracuse belong more to the past than Chichén Itzá? Does Chichén Itzá belong more to the past than Auschwitz?

Cows, scrawny soft-eyed animals, made room for me to pass by. Shortly afterward came an Indian, brightly clothed, a machete in his hand. If he feels like it, he could kill me and I'd never be found.

He stopped and said, "Ah, just an Indian."

The tone of voice matched exactly, the disdain, the heartlessness.

He made a gesture with the machete like chopping off a head. Looked at me expectantly.

He's giving me the decision over W.'s life. The empress who turns her thumb up or down. Turn it down, toward the dirt, into the dirt, down with all murderers. The Indian looked at me, I shook my head.

Disappointed, he walked on.

An opportunity missed. How often do you meet someone who offers himself for that?

For that. Yes, for that. For murder. Don't try to think it away, don't think around it or beyond it. Murder. I murder. He has murdered. Because he murdered, I will murder. I or the Indian carrying out the contract. Division of effort into clean and dirty. Meantime the word's gotten around that that excuse won't work. Are you allowed to murder a murderer? Who allows, who forbids it? You're not allowed to. But

the W.'s make our morals *kaputt.* Evil is infectious. As you
to me, so I to you, an eye for an eye. Nonsense. During the
war, perhaps, when they were still in the middle of it. Not
any longer. Or maybe still? Nothing but uncertainty. "Yes,
shoot him," said Alyosha Karamazov, after Ivan had asked
whether the general, who'd let his dogs tear the little boy
apart, should be shot rather than relieved of his command.
And took his words back right away: "I said something stupid." Something stupid? Or not? Do it by counting off but-
tons or pulling off petals, silly as Gretchen, the way we all
were when we were twenty. As if anything would change with
W.'s death. As if Eichmann's death changed anything. A
world-historical joke: his office will be superfluous during
the next genocide – what occupied those diligent bureaucrats
for four years a computer can take care of in a few seconds.

The W.'s of the past are hardly dangerous any longer.
They've killed enough, want a little peace and quiet, a little
house and a little garden so they can plant flowers. Even I
plant flowers. With each hole I dig for one, I think I'm digging my own grave. Standing beside me is someone with a
loaded gun. C'mon, let's go, get a move on! Faster! If I'm
not fast enough he'll hit me. Don't hit me, just don't hit me.
Don't smash my head in with the rifle butt. Rather be shot.
A bullet in the back of the head as the ultimate luxury. But
perhaps something will happen before that. You never know.
The king's messenger on horseback. It worked for Dos-
toyevsky. The only case I know of. Pre-computer age. When
the word "mercy" still crossed people's lips.

Above me, a frightened cry. A huge, yellow bird. Whirring
in the air, golden spirals, carried up over the treetops and
away.

Showered again, changed underwear, it's oppressively

82

humid, not a breath of air, to the south a wall of clouds towers up. The shadows have lengthened. No danger of encountering W. and the tour group any more.

Past the hotel again, to the ruins, show my admission card, "we're closing in fifty minutes," then up onto the pyramid called El Castillo. Ninety one steps, each one so narrow that your foot will fit only if it's turned sideways and so steep that I have to put my bag and Rolleiflex on each step ahead of me. Four times 91 makes 364, add the platform on top and it makes 365, a complete year. Being masters of astronomy, the calendar, and mathematics doesn't keep you from murdering. And the calendar stones, copied in thin, stamped silver, hang from the ears of female tourists. The souvenir culture. Old symbol becomes new symbol. The word "sign" is better. Everything's a sign, from miniskirt and Beatles' haircut to computer formulas. Guernica and electronic music. Happenings and the equation for the extension of space. But mathematics doesn't keep you from murdering. What does?

On top, puffing. Climbed too fast. Catch my breath on the north side of the square temple. Sacrifices were carried out here, too. The steps were good training for the executioners, you have to be young and fit to be able to rip the heart out of someone's breast. But what did the victims feel like on the way up? Fear-sweat is cold, the sweat from climbing is warm. Torture steps. For me it was like shoveling my own grave. Those are my experiences, that's the life that W. gave me as a gift.

Around the platform to the east, then to the south, then suddenly I heard dance music coming from a phonograph or radio; as I came around to the west side, I saw the men. Three of them on little folding chairs, playing cards. A stool

83

for a table, a transistor radio standing beside it. They were young, around thirty, and were wearing stylish, short-sleeved sport shirts.

"My ace on your Jack," said one in German. Triumphantly. "Victoria! Victoria!"

"I knock," said the other one. Then the first one: "Oh, God, said Agatha, and I'm still a virgin."

The third one noticed me, alerted his friends; the one who'd come out with the business about Agatha looked a little embarrassed. "C'mon, the ol' lady didn't understand."

"What's she doing up here?"

"Are we talkin' about old ladies or playing *skat*? Time for three more hands before sunset."

"We'll be rid of her by then. She certainly didn't heave herself up here to enjoy nature. Only we Germans have any sense for that."

With the riding crop, a slap across the face. The slender Dutch Jewish boy lets loose a scream and the man with the whip in his hand – not W., W. doesn't use the whip – "You filthy Jews, we'll teach you to hide. We Germans don't have much patience with slackers."

But for sunsets. Still "we Germans," always "we Germans."

"No, I'm not in favor of the military." He fixes my television set or my faucet or pushes the travelers' checks across the counter toward me at the bank so I can sign them, one by one, long enough for a conversation, and he tells me how he loves to lie in the Mediterranean sun and that he goes to the soccer game every Saturday, and every Sunday morning he washes his car and is looking for a woman who's pretty and frugal – or has one already – and then comes the inevitable sentence, "We Germans are . . ." "We Germans have . . ." "We Germans." And I nod, find it completely *in Ordnung*, "We

Germans." In Germany, that just runs off me like water, but not here, not among the ruins where the Maya murdered.

And again the urge to flee, but the sunset gets in my way; above the greenish-black fabric of the jungle, it flames out of the clouds, red and golden, rust and orange, the blast of trumpets that caused the walls of Jericho to come tumbling down.

"Trump is the soul of the game."

They don't need to stuff their ears with wax, the song of the sirens is lost in the blaring of the radio, everything beautiful and everything horrible is familiar to them.

Corpses on the television screen at suppertime, soldiers lean over a prisoner lying on the ground, you can't see exactly what they're doing to him, but you get the idea, ruins of a blown-up house, the mangled body of a child. Before you go to sleep in a warm bed, a quick look at the newspaper, the "photo of the year," a human being, tied to a tank, dragged to his death.

"Triumph, the puddle is spreading."

Reddish tones devoured by gold, rays of gold thrusting over the tangle of branches, walls, card players, *jubilate*, intoxicated with joy, the best of all possible worlds, the color of angels, then spreading strangely, *Gloria in excelsis Deo*, for the glory of God in heaven Cortez and his men tortured and murdered. The Indians took the Spaniards for white gods, the Spaniards the Indians for black devils. Two-fold error made the slaughter easier.

"Whose deal?"

"Always the one who asks."

In Spain, Cortez owned a showroom where he displayed Indians. At the same time, dog handlers were combing Mexico for hidden Indians. Paid by the head.

"Carp in herb butter."

They had dog handlers in the Gestapo and for every one they brought in they got three guldens.

"The little ones pull in the big ones."

Stories, old ones, that's the way it was, no it wasn't. Stories give nothing back, not our insanity, no one normal any longer, persecutor and persecuted, each one beyond the pale, intoxicated by power, by misfortune, the hideous desperation, life at its most intensive.

"A spade, the gaudy woodpecker."

W. whistled. But do I know that I didn't whistle, too, sometime or other? And if I didn't whistle, then I laughed, no one can live for years without laughing. And someone whose time was up must have heard me.

"Heart-ily did the Germans laugh and blow their horns."

Stop talking about laughing, stop, stop.

"For a grand slam pull an ace; otherwise, shut your face."

Shut your face is good. Comfortable in any case.

Everything beneath us in deep shadow; we alone in light.

The gold has dissolved, the western sky is shrouded by pale yellow silk, far below, the red ball. How often have I seen it sink since we sat, at the age of sixteen, in the monopteros and watched it submerge behind the trees to the right of the spires of the Church of St. Louis? "And already he has departed for foreign lands, whose people still honor him." Back when we still believed in pious peoples. Now it was gone; gray coolness rose up from below.

"Won and done!"

The swiftly descending dusk of the tropics. It was high time to go back down.

As I sat over breakfast in the main building, it began to rain. Oh, what do I mean "rain"? Rain is what it does at home, sometimes it even pours, but here it was a waterfall crashing down from the sky. Impossible to walk the fifty yards to my bungalow. Endless breakfast, another cup of coffee, one more piece of toast, it's already eleven and my bus goes at three, I'll skip lunch, supper on the plane, probably not very fancy, it's only an hour to New Orleans, they're not going to put themselves out. But at least there'll be a couple sandwiches. I wish I were already there. Had enough of the Mayas and Toltecs and vultures. Yes, even enough of the vultures. Too bad the lady from the bus isn't here. She'd be delighted.

At half past eleven it let up; I took off my shoes and stockings and ran through the puddles to my room. Lay down on the bed, didn't feel like reading, didn't feel like doing anything.

Just want to lie here. That's not a death wish. No longer that wild longing for nothingness. When the passions burn down, even that dies out. Just want to lie here, forget. Forget everything. Forget W. By wanting to forget him, I drag him into the light. His voice. His moustache. His pipe. A shag pipe. What's a shag pipe, anyway? A tobacco is called shag. Or a certain cut. Sounds like Sherlock Holmes, Baker Street, Watson, *The Hound of the Baskervilles.* One of my favorite books when I was a child. *The Speckled Band.* No, don't lose the thread. His sport jacket. His uniform jacket, his cap at an angle, with its death's head. He was a handsome young man. Would I have if he wanted to? Probably. What's forbidden's attractive. The absurd danger. A death warrant for two, if you're caught in bed together. In the twentieth century. Still that way in South Africa. Well, maybe not death, but prison and whipping. And in a few states in the U.S.A, marriage between black and white was forbidden up until a little while ago.

Sometimes he took Jewish women up to his room. For

a quarter of an hour. *Passer* is what it's called in French brothels. *Passer* and then sent back downstairs to the others who are waiting to be taken away. "Ah, a Jewish *schickse.*" Completely unmoved. Nothing moved him unless it had something to do directly with him. He's bad. Crude. But probably no cruder and no worse than many others whom fate saved from the S S. Whatever he did then – he wouldn't understand it later. Later, it's just incomprehensible.

Should he be condemned anyway, if it's him? Life in prison? How good it is that I don't have to make the choice. I don't want to decide any more. So then, is everything I'm saying, thinking, doing, merely lamenting the fact? Too little! I decide. I'm going to bring charges. *J'accuse, j'accuse, j'accuse.*

I stood up, went out. The rain had stopped. The fragrance had become stronger, an insane fragrance. A hundred thousand tuberoses. Sickly sweet.

Dark clouds race from west to east. Soon it's going to rain again. How am I going to get to the bus? Is there a taxi in this damned place? I'd better go over to the hotel while it's dry.

I picked up my coat, my small suitcase, shoulder bag, and Rolleiflex. Paid the bill in the main building. "*Au revoir,*" said the woman manager; it sounded like the password in some conspiracy against the Americans.

The street was empty, there weren't even any iguanas playing in the ditch. Only the circling vultures. A swarm of them flew so low above me that I could see their naked heads.

A hundred yards from the hotel the first drops started to fall. My baggage kept me from running. I hurried, stumbled, but managed to reach the building still relatively dry.

A sort of anteroom, the stone monstrosities of the Toltecs

were reproduced in brightly painted wood; in one corner was a shop with souvenirs.

Then the lobby, a long tunnel, open toward the garden, which is pleasant because the tobacco smell is wafted away, and unpleasant because the dampness makes its way in, all exotic within limits, specifically designed to accommodate the maximum number of people during bad weather.

An empty chair; finally I can put down my suitcase and Rolleiflex; the bag I keep on my lap.

To my right the three Germans are sitting around a table playing cards. "Whose deal?" "Always the one who asks." To the left a fat woman is sitting in a wicker chair with her legs spread so far apart that I can see how her tight, gray cotton panties bite into the reddish flesh of her thighs. She's having a conversation with a skinny person who's sitting beside her, wearing a flowered summer dress and a white straw hat with a pink ribbon around it.

But where is W.? I can't see him. Is he in bed with the blond?

"There are no civilians in Viet Nam," says the fat woman.

"Even the children have guns. And the women are armed when they go into the fields."

"No civilians," comes the echo from the skinny one.

"So no one can accuse us of killing civilians."

"You said it."

"We ought to be tougher with them. Destroy Hanoi. And if nothing else works, then an atom bomb. Instead of constantly risking the lives of our soldiers."

I push my chair back, bump against a knee, "Oh, sorry!" and now, at the far end of the lobby, half hidden by the fat woman, I see W. sitting on a sofa beside the blond, his pipe in his hand. Now and then he uses the pipe as a pointer, or as a head-scratcher – something a real smoker would never do –

it's not lit, wasn't lit yesterday, he's a miserable actor, doesn't use his props the right way. Doesn't take it seriously enough. Probably hasn't taken anything seriously his entire life.

"This rain," says the fat woman. "Horrible. For this we paid all that money. Doesn't even cool off afterward. I'm so hot I could explode. Where's the cologne?"

The skinny one rummages hastily through her handbag. "Don't be so slow. I'm about to choke!"

The skinny one finds the bottle. The fat one shakes some of the leathery-smelling liquid onto a handkerchief and wipes her face with it.

I can't stand Russian Leather. Should I move farther away? Closer to W.? I certainly wouldn't learn any more than I did yesterday. Harmless conversation with his protégé. As far as I can judge, he speaks English without an accent. That's no alibi. Anyone who's gifted at languages can learn to do that. I'd have to get him to speak German. But even if he spoke it perfectly, I wouldn't be any further along. Not even if he admitted to being W. "Yes, dear lady," he'd say, "I was with the SS. But note carefully, it was the Waffen-SS. Wounded in the east, hit in the leg, you'll recall that I limped a little back in those days. I had the misfortune to be sent back to Amsterdam to guard internees until my wound healed completely. Do you think that was fun for me? But what *was* I supposed to do? Orders are orders. Refusal would've meant the end of me. To tell the truth, the idea never occurred to me. First of all, someone would have had to tell me that there even was such a thing as refusing to follow orders. And if I had known, and did refuse, would there have been any sense to the sacrifice? There were plenty of replacements. Basically you've got to look out for yourself and I wasn't made to be a martyr. I've always behaved decently. Did you ever see me hit anyone back then, dear lady? Always polite, that was my

motto even then, everything runs much more smoothly
with politeness. 'What good does it do you,' I said to myself,
'to scare people? Your job is see to it that the apparatus
functions without friction right up to the time they're transported away. What happens afterward is none of your business. But as long as you're in charge of these people, you'll
make it work better with a friendly word.' Wasn't that easy,
imposing discipline on such an undisciplined bunch. That's
something you yourself have to admit, dear lady. With the
exception of the ones who'd served in the German Army,
the so-called front-line soldiers from the first war, every one
of those lawyers, doctors, and merchants did whatever he
wanted, not to mention the Amsterdamers from the Jewish
district, the little shopkeepers, diamond cutters, tailors, and
Talmud scholars. A real passel of pigs. Totally without understanding for the fact that discipline is necessary when so
many people are crammed together. How did I get to Mexico, dear lady? Simple. I had my nose full. Things were just
too confining for me back there. This continent has freedom
and wide-open spaces. Absolutely right for my mother's son.
And being a tour guide is far from the worst thing in the
world. An educated profession, fits with my inclinations,
you get to meet people. The years in between, dear lady, the
ones after 1943? Wound healed, back to the front, in France,
fortunately, though the invasion wasn't exactly a laughing
matter, either. After the big dust-up, a year in England as a
prisoner, a year's worth of language lessons for free. Can I
help you with anything else, dear lady?"

"I don't believe you. You were at Auschwitz. Where else
would you have gotten the expression 'The Black Wall?'"

"Black Wall? What bothers you about that, dear lady?
Certainly not that I make it a point to mention 'The Black
Wall of the Toltecs' during my tours? That wall is black.

Didn't you notice? And built by the Toltecs, not the Mayas, which is what it says in every art book and obviously that has to be brought to the public's attention by any conscientious guide. Don't hold an innocent remark against me. Astonishing, the things you have to watch out for."

"I don't believe you. You were at Auschwitz."

"And if I'd been there, dear lady, it would have been the same bad luck that I had in Amsterdam. An unlucky guy, you might say, at least during the war, because later things worked out more satisfactorily. Assuming, then, that someone or other might claim to have seen me at the place whose name I'd rather not mention, say on the ramp or in an office or at roll call, that would be a long way from meaning that I'd tortured people there. As was quite easily proved in the cases of Boger and Kaduk. Sent people to the gas chamber? Decided which ones? Still assuming I was there, what else could I have done, dear lady? A pilot pushes a button that drops the bomb, a worker in a poison gas factory puts a deadly chemical into a retort. An SS man at a camp makes a selection. For sabotage and strikes the penalty is the firing squad. And when you get down to it, selection means, as the word itself says, not just annihilation but also rescue. You know, dear lady, that I was not insensitive to the beauty of young Jewish women. Again, assuming that's the way it was, I would have done my job."

"I don't believe you. First you slept with the girls, then you sent them to the gas."

"You know, dear lady, how powerless the individual was. *Unterscharführer*? Means nothing. Twenty-three years old, had taken an oath of allegiance, brought up to be obedient, even when I was at home we children had to keep our noses clean. Beatings for bad grades. Behave yourself, we were told. Sit straight. Hands on the table. Keep your mouth shut. A

German boy doesn't cry. Don't be a coward. Grit your teeth. The greatest good our fatherland. Betrayed by the Jews. Stab in the back. World Jewry, our enemy. Exploiting us. Break out of capitalist serfdom. The degradation of Versailles. Schlageter, Our Hero. With heart and hand. No more beautiful death in all the world. Their cry like a thunderous roar. Hoist the flag. Your loyalty is your honor. That's drilled into you and it sticks, dear lady. Your loyalty is your honor. For the sake of loyalty, do your duty. Would have done it even there, if that place had been my fate."

"I don't believe you. You were there."

"Perhaps dear lady, perhaps not. Who doesn't occasionally forget a place he's been? Who doesn't occasionally think he knows a place when he doesn't? Even the best brain can fail you and mistake hearsay for real experience. I prefer to limit myself to what I can see and what's unambiguous – to the present. Tour guide in Chichén Itzá, employee of Barbachano, not badly paid, and, if I may mention it, a Mexican passport in my pocket. Those are facts. Everything else is speculation. But I'll do you the favor, dear lady, of looking at the situation from another point of view. Let's assume that there was a man of my name, my build, and background at the spot where you insist on placing me; was that me? Are you still the same one, to whom a young soldier said, after a long night, that you had the most beautiful eyes? Look in the mirror, dear lady. By which I don't mean to say that your eyes have become ugly, but they're not beautiful – certainly not the most beautiful – any more. Being beautiful requires something more than external attractiveness and, in your case, that something more came about through passion, pain, and sorrow, through a wildness that made their gentle gray-blue all the more charming. Only the somewhat faded color is left. You've adapted."

93

The gong sounded.

"Finally," said the fat woman, "I'm dying of hunger. And I'm sure there won't be anything other than rice with some spicy thing. I swear, the first time I see a real steak, I'm gonna cry for joy. Can you at least help me out of this awful chair?"

The skinny woman pulled for all she was worth; finally she succeeded. The view of W. was clear. Someone around him must have said something funny; he was laughing so hard that he was shaking.

"Yes, indeed, dear lady, you've adapted the way anyone who survives adapts. Pain becomes skepticism, indignation changes to uneasiness, and when I see you this way, on a trip that costs an arm and a leg, well-dressed, interested in people and art, I'll bet that you've not only adapted, but for the most part are pretty much satisfied with this world, which has improved for you, of course, but for the greater part of humanity is just as bad as ever. You protest against whatever you don't like, against atom bombs, the Viet Nam War, and apartheid. Protests are fun. Yes, really, you'd probably feel something was missing if there were nothing more to protest against. But, of the young woman who wanted to set the world on fire out of despair, there's nothing left. And here you are trying to convince me that I'm the same person who guarded the captured Jews until their journey into death and, beyond that, you're trying to stick me with the role of a murderer at that place. Whatever happened there, it wasn't me."

"I don't believe you."

"What do you want, anyway, dear lady? To send me to prison? Because for you, punishment and revenge are what protects society? Why are you persecuting me, someone who was just a good soldier, someone who took orders, death's fellow traveler? We, the Germans – and in this instance, dear lady, I'd like to count us both among them – have had

94

considerable sympathy for death for a long time. The art of living doesn't count for much back home. From which it follows that letting others live by their lights isn't held in such high regard, either. The land of romanticism. Romanticism in love, romanticism in politics. The blood-spattered blue flower. Unfailingly bound to illusions. Be so kind as to remember, dear lady, November '32. The theater on Gärtnerplatz. They're putting on some operetta or other, you're sitting with your escort in the very front row, the first act is over and – as was the fashion then – down comes the curtain with the advertisements on it, then you hear a voice behind you saying, 'I find these advertisements repulsive, they ruin any sense of illusion for me.' You're shocked that there's somebody who can be transported into the world of illusion by the piece of fluff that you've just seen, who doesn't want to awaken from the raspberry-lemonade dream. You turn around, annoyed, and see – scarcely a yard away from you, done up in pompador and mustache like some heavy from a B movie – the face of the man whom the Germans call the *Führer*, stare into his cold, penetrating eyes, into the eyes of your death and you take the arm of your beloved escort and drag him along, out of the theater, pack your bags that very same hour in order to put the ocean between you and the operetta-enchanted monstrosity. However, that's not what you did, dear lady. You did, indeed, leave the theater right then and there, but as soon as you were out on the street, you whispered to your friend that now you were completely relieved, the German people were not going to be taken in by that mediocre clown with the face of a sleazy con man. *Your* blue flower, the reasonable German people. Fit in with the way you saw things. Even you didn't want to see the curtain come down, you wished things would just go on the same way, eternally, You see, dear lady, your 'I don't believe you' is sticking in your throat. You're beginning to believe me. And why not? Basically we're two peas in a pod. At your first carnival ball, you were seventeen, you danced with a fellow costumed as a villain, sat on his lap, and didn't object when he said, 'You're an attractive Jewish girl and I march with the SA. Keep pace with the best of them.' How do you know it wasn't me that you kissed and allowed to fondle your breasts? Forbidden games, dear lady, playing at Romeo and Juliet, just that we didn't love each other; what we did then, under the protection of the nightingale, was *l'art pour l'art* and we both enjoyed it. The tenderest of enemies, someone needs to put a stop to the Montagues, not sweet Romeo. You my Jewess, I your Nazi, till the song of the lark. But even in the cold, wintery light of morning, when I took you home, you didn't call the police. Permit me the additional observation that I was very impressed by your father's house, although I only got to see it from the outside before I went home to my blue-collar neighborhood, where I shared a room in a small apartment with my two brothers. The social difference was too great. Without my nationalistic upbringing, I would have been marching with the Red Front. Gotta march, doesn't matter with whom. In lock-step against loneliness. Anyone who wears a wide belt or even just a uniform jacket, he's someone. Being someone is important. *What* doesn't matter. The what is something for finer folks. Like you, dear lady. Because you had money, you could pick and choose and you chose to the left, out of sympathy for the poor, belief in social justice – and why not, as far as I'm concerned. But marching wasn't your bit and you weren't available to break up political rallies and certainly not for anything that involved fistfights or bloodshed. Remember, once again, Paris, 1931, an outdoor café on the Champs Elysées, spring, you in a blue and white checked suit, without a hat. You never wore a hat. What your friend was wearing is no longer certain, you were just looking at his face, not his suit. His voice was slightly husky as he said, 'Actually, it's high time to do something about the Nazis. I've been thinking about joining the *Reichsbanner*.' I grant you, he made your job easy, with his 'actually' and 'I've been thinking,' so it wasn't necessary to use all the powers of persuasion at your command to get him to give up his half-baked plan. That was the moment of *your* guilt. You had enough understanding and imagination to know what would happen if every loving woman spoke the way you did. Guilt against guilt. Who's going to weigh that? One justice against a different one, *faites votre jeu.* So the thing happened that neither of us can understand today, that no one understands. It came, turned into the present, and when it was no longer able to be that, it was no longer anything. Our past is not one that can be lived with and since we're living, it can't have existed. Even those blind chickens I herd through the ruins to earn my daily bread have something they can think back on. Not us. We dare not, will not, cannot. Either-or. You've said "or," so you have to finish what you've started, study the stock reports, think about what kind of a car you're going to drive, what trip you're going to take, buy clothes, buy books, swim in the Mediterranean, ski on the Diavolezza, mow the lawn, act your way through flirtations that become more melancholy year by year, hang onto friendships that are steadily diminishing. Finish what you started, be consistent. Travel to London when the Bolshoi's performing there, to Antibes to see Picasso, to see Léger in Biot. Take a detour to see a Romanesque church, know where, what, and when, read, look, read, listen to music, watch television, get to really know history, be able to go through art museums and torture museums without a guide, have opinions, express opinions, talk about the trial of Socrates, and about the Bogers and Kaduks, beat about the bush when you write, like a cat sneaking around the hot oven, because there's nothing you can write about nothing, gravy spots on the paper and burned paws. Finishing what you started has to be learned, being consistent has to be practiced, *exercise*. Up to the barre, right leg, left leg, ankles up, ankles down, up on your toes. Now! Those dreams of choosing the right course? Demand that they jump through burning hoops, without getting their hearts singed. Sink your face into the dog's fur and let it be licked by his tongue – the last remaining tenderness – and don't think about the fact that the dear creature's ancestors tracked down fleeing Indians, tore them apart, and devoured them. Finish what you started, be consistent. You've applied yourself, developed further, but never got your master's certificate. And the raging fear that sometime, in a hospital bed, in a ditch alongside the road, will come the persistent remorse that you didn't choose the other alternative. The hour of truth, and the truth farther away than ever. Who could tell you the truth? What is your truth? Fleeting images, changeable as clouds – camels, weasels, whales, while you're tormenting yourself deciding which they are, they've already turned into something else. Everything flowing. Your sadness and your joy, your I-hate-the-world and your I-love-the-world, tired of life, hungry for life, the widow's black veil over your face, sniffing the smell of blossoms, earth, semen, ski wax, full to the point of nausea and still can't get enough to eat, yes, yes, and no, no to revenge, to forgiveness, and then you lose your nerve because of a couple of skulls chiseled into stone. Go ahead, take the images at their word. It makes me sick, hearing accusations all the time. Okay, it was horrible, what Las Casas described and what the witnesses said about

Boger. The Spanish didn't believe it, the Germans don't believe it. Those things are done but not believed. Who believes in James Bond and the comic strips? Not even ten-year-olds. They sat there, brought in class by class, slouched in the front seats during that trial, picked their noses, elbowed their neighbors, and only listened when atrocities were being mentioned. Education to become citizens. That's your democracy for you. And just think of this: there was a lawyer who was involved in the trial from the very beginning – a whole year, three days every week. Then he happened to walk down a street where someone had been run over. There was still blood on the macadam. He later admitted that not until that moment had he been able to imagine what it had been like where Boger was in charge. A bit of fluid convinced him more than all the words uttered during an entire year. Do you need hearts torn out of the breast for information? A black wall as stimulation for your imagination? That's too simple. We both know how things are, know all about nothingness, which we don't understand with our heads but with our nerves, while we're awake, asleep, with every heartbeat. That's what distinguishes us from the others, that's our common ground, where we belong to the same lodge."

W. and I were sitting in the lobby alone. He was reading a magazine and playing with his cold pipe. I pulled a cigarette out of my handbag. At that moment, he looked over, stood up, and came over to me, pushing aside the few chairs that stood in his way. My hand trembled as it held the cigarette. Standing in front of me, he flicked his lighter and held it toward me as it flamed up. After my cigarette was lit, he gave me a supercilious look, turned around and walked out into the garden. Over the sound of the falling rain I could hear him whistling softly to himself.

And I? A Witness to Pain

At the request of my hosts, I'm telling a small group of cultivated, unusually interested people about my time as a fugitive in Holland. It's easy for me to describe objectively, completely without emotion, my hiding place behind the row of bookcases.

Then a woman who's been sitting across from me, watching me intently, says, "You must have been horribly afraid the whole time." I nod noncommittally in her direction, without agreeing, without contradicting.

It's impossible for me to say, "I wasn't afraid, not for a single moment. That's the absolute truth."

After the murder of my husband Edgar at Mauthausen, everything was a matter of such complete indifference that there was neither time nor space in which to be afraid.

A curious, floating condition of not-standing-on-earth.

I wore my fearlessness (not courage – it had absolutely nothing to do with courage) like a magic cape. It concealed me, made me invulnerable.

I often got into extraordinarily difficult situations. I always came away without a scratch.

I realize immediately that I can't tell these people that I wasn't afraid.

I don't want them to take me for a liar, or a braggart, or for a stupid goose who couldn't recognize danger.

After Edgar's murder there was nothing I wished for more than death. I wouldn't, couldn't bring it upon myself, because I didn't want to do to my mother, who was also living in exile in Holland, what had just been done to me, because at the time I'd already sensed what later proved to be correct: the nearly seventy-year-old woman would not have had the least chance of surviving without me.

What I couldn't do to myself was something only the Germans could, and it hardly mattered what cruel way they picked (and there I was under no illusions). If I could just simply stop living, mourning for Edgar, and longing for him. But my mother – full of life, quick, witty, courageous – was not going to end up in a concentration camp. (Nobody knew anything about gas chambers back then.)

But what a miracle it was that we both made it through became clear to me in its full extent only much later, after the war, when I was forced to realize something which is still so difficult to comprehend, that in fact *all* Jews were marked for annihilation and in great measure *were* killed.

The afternoon I was in Munich talking about going into hiding fell right in the midst of the weeks when I was thinking hard about a book I wanted to write with the title "Aftershocks."

At the same time I recognize clearly that there's nothing in our lives nowadays that couldn't be considered an aftershock.

Starting with Kohl's attempt to weasel his way out using words about the mercy of a late birth and on to Jenninger's notorious television speech of the ninth of November, during which I became aware that its content hurt me less than the monotonous, indifferent way in which he delivered it.

Everything around me is an aftershock because the Hitler

era left behind such obvious traces that no one who was living then, and probably only a handful of those born later, can avoid them. And I? Well, I'm beginning to think about the aftershocks that have to do with me.

Would I have written without the persecution? Yes, absolutely. I've been writing since my fifteenth year and never wanted to do anything else. Would I have written differently? Certainly. And I would have become a quite different person if Edgar had remained with me.

I'm still alive, but my fearlessness came to an end after the war. I never was and still am not excessively timid, but my magic cape is gone. It's superfluous. There is, at least for the present and for me, no longer an Auschwitz in our part of the world. On the other hand, probably just like any other person, I'm afraid of illness or weakness that might make me completely dependent.

But how did I manage to go on living with all that I know? I think about those who couldn't, about Jean Améry, Primo Levi, Paul Celan, and now Bruno Bettelheim as well.

The difference is that they were in the camps; I wasn't. During the month and a half that Edgar was in Mauthausen – an eternity during which I received two letters from him that held out no hope – during that time and even much later, I believed that I'd experienced everything along with him, all the fears, every torment, every pain that came from abuse, and the impotent despair over the violent death of his comrades.

That belief was taken from me some time ago – an aftershock. Primo Levi described the camps in such minute detail that the unimaginable became a concrete picture.

For forty years I'd imagined that I was a witness and that made it possible for me to live the way I have. I'm no longer a witness. I didn't know a thing. Whenever I read Primo Levi, I realize that I couldn't really visualize a concentration camp. My imagination wasn't sick enough.

I wasn't together with Edgar at Mauthausen, as I sometimes – maybe often, maybe even always – believed at the time.

He'd already been dead for fourteen days when I got the news in the form of one of my letters which came back with the notation written in red pencil, "Addressee unknown," and, beside it, the death-rune. What the death-rune looked like I learned from friends who got back their letter to their son the same way, together with the notification of his death from the Jewish Council (there still was one in 1941). I got the notification from the Jewish Council two weeks later. Edgar was dead and I didn't know it. I wasn't with him at Mauthausen. I was sitting in the relative safety of our apartment in Amsterdam where his gray summer coat was still hanging in the clothes closet beside the door. I could bury my head in it whenever things got really bad.

As an epigraph for a love story – Edgar's and my story, which I wrote two years later hiding on the attic stairs, the only place where I could be alone – as an epigraph I'd chosen a verse by a long-forgotten poet of the twenties, Klabund: "Forgive me. I did something that is fitting for God alone to do – took your hand for my hand, your heart for mine." And now that heart had been still for weeks already, but mine went on beating persistently, irregularly, and, as usual, a little too fast, as it has already for fifty years. I hadn't known that he was dead. Nonsense to think that one could feel such a thing. Each day he was in that accursed place I should have been able to say to myself and anyone who wanted to hear it or didn't want to hear it, "I know he's dead." And if I'd said it as well on the day that later turned out to have been the day he died, I might have drawn the conclusion that I'd really felt it. But I didn't. I've always left that sort of thing to others, to those who play with mental telepathy, the ones who get carried away by mysticism or find something to hold on to in some religion or other, no matter how far out it might be, and believe in the divine order of the world and being reunited in a life after death.

How was I to know about his horrible death (even today I still don't know how it happened) and his hardly less horrible life in the concentration camp? That's something I have to realize, and, as well, that my often expressed claim of having been a witness has evaporated.

Maybe I've remained alive simply because I didn't witness enough. I witnessed the persecution, but not the deportations, really, let alone the horrors of the concentration camps. Primo Levi writes (and by "survivors" he means those who've survived the concentration camps): "We, the survivors, are not only a vanishingly small minority, but an abnormal one, people who by forsaking their duties, or by means of their cleverness or their luck, never reached the deepest point of the abyss. Whoever did reach it, whoever caught sight of the head of Medusa, was unable to return again or was struck mute." Despite this confession, Primo Levi took his own life. What am I to say – I who held on to the illusion that I was one with another human being who had seen the head of Medusa?

All phantasy, a distorted, awful dream. Now I know quite precisely what happened in the concentration camps – in reality, not merely in my overheated imagination.

I've written a couple of books. They told people about the senselessness, the humiliation, about the guilty consciences of those who survived, and again and again about the pain that never lets up.

At first no one wanted to read them. Then they were accepted – after a very long time.

Aftershock? I don't know.

But not a story for the book I was going to write.

Not a story at all.

Words or passages given in English or French in the original German edition have been italicized.

page 28   "God Punish England": From Ernst Lissauer's poem "*Hassgesang Gegen England*" ("Hymn of Hatred Against England"), composed in 1914. A censor might not have found the phrase at all ridiculous since it was used on stamps and on postcards during World War I. Lissauer's promising literary career suffered because of postwar criticism of the poem. He emigrated to Vienna, where he is buried in the Jewish cemetery.

page 39   "Nibble, nibble, little mousie": From the Grimm brothers' fairy tale "Hansel and Gretel."

page 40   "Once again your silent splendor fills field and forest": From Goethe's poem "*An den Mond*" ("To the Moon"). Uncle Maxie's misquotation is minor.

page 73   "a Grand Guignol play": The Grand Guignol Theater in Paris (1897–1962) specialized in grisly horror productions, with such special effects as the gouged-out eye trick.

page 73   "Boger's swing": A torture device, which, according to most accounts, was used as follows: the victim was forced to embrace his lower legs with his hands, which were then tied together. A metal rod was thrust through the loops formed by knees and forearms; then the ends of the rod were attached to chains hanging from the ceiling, by means of which the victim was hoisted off the floor and beaten while being rotated around the bar. At the Frankfurt Auschwitz trials conducted by the German government, the SS non-commissioned officer Wilhelm Boger received a life sentence plus fifteen years for his role in torturing concentration camp inmates.

page 73   Lili Tofler was executed at Auschwitz for smuggling a letter to a fellow inmate.

page 74   "*Scharführer*": An SS rank equivalent to the regular army rank of staff sergeant; "*Unterscharführer*" is equivalent to sergeant; "*Hauptsturmführer*" is equivalent to an army captain.

page 81   "latomias": Stone prisons in ancient Syracuse.

page 84   "skat": A card game related to bridge.

page 85   "... stuff their ears with wax": In book XII of *The Odyssey*, Odysseus stuffs his sailors' ears with kneaded beeswax in order to prevent them from hearing the sirens' songs.

page 86   "monopteros": A Greek-style round columned temple in Munich's English Garden.

page 86   "And already he has departed for foreign lands": An approximation of lines from the poem "*Sonnenuntergang*" ("Sunset") by the German Romantic poet Friedrich Hölderlin (1770-1843), describing the sun god's departure for other parts of the world.

page 92   Oswald Kaduk, like Boger, was another infamous SS guard at Auschwitz. The Soviets sentenced him to twenty-five years at hard labor, then pardoned him after ten years; he was rearrested and retried by the West German government and sentenced to life imprisonment for murder. He was released in 1989 and died in 1997.

page 93   "Schlagater, Our Hero": Albert Leo Schlagater was a former World War I soldier executed by the French for sabotage during their occupation of the Rhineland. The Nazis made him into a hero, naming a navy training ship and a fighter squadron in his honor.

page 95   "... a man whom the Germans call the Führer": This description of Hitler and the narrator's disbelief that such a mediocre clown could ever come to power are taken directly from Grete Weil's real-life experience described in her memoir *Leb Ich Denn, Wenn Andere Leben*.

page 97   "*Reichsbanner*": A left-wing paramilitary group dating from 1924.

page 98   "Las Casas": Bartolomé de Las Casas, a Spanish-born priest who emigrated to the Indies. His horror at the murderous mistreatment of the natives led him to write his *Brevisima Relación de la Destrucción de Las Indias* ("Brief Account of the Destruction of the Indies").

page 104 "Kohl's attempt" occurred during German Chancellor Helmut Kohl's visit, in January of 1984, to Israel, when he hoped, as representative of a "new Germany," to open an era of understanding between the two countries that would be less constrained by Germany's past. Unfortunately, Kohl, who was fifteen years old at the end of World War II, chose to begin his speech before the Knesset with the pronouncement, "I am speaking to you as one who could not be implicated in the guilt of the Nazi era, thanks to the grace of a late birth..."

page 104 "Jenninger's notorious television speech" refers to the address given by Philipp Jenninger, president of the German federal legislative body, the Bundestag, on the fiftieth anniversary of the Reichskrystallnacht, the murderous rampage loosed against the Jews in 1938. The speech resulted in public outrage not because its content was in any way inaccurate or exculpatory, but because of, as Grete Weil points out, the dry, monotone fashion in which he spoke. Jenninger resigned his post but remained active as a diplomat thereafter.

page 105 Jean Améry, Primo Levi, Paul Celan, and Bruno Bettelheim all survived concentration camps; all eventually took their own lives.

ABOUT THE AUTHOR

GRETE WEIL was one of twentieth-century Germany's most celebrated writers. Born Margarete Elisabeth Dispeker in 1906, she grew up in Munich and studied German literature in preparation for a career in writing. In 1932 she married Edgar Weil, a member of the Munich Kammerspiele theater staff. When he was briefly arrested by the Nazis, Grete Weil abandoned her university studies and took up photography as a means of earning a living after the couple emigrated to the Netherlands. During the German occupation, Edgar Weil was caught in a street raid in Amsterdam and perished in the Mauthausen Concentration camp. After Grete Weil found a hiding place for her widowed mother, enabling her to survive the war, the author herself went into hiding in 1943 for the duration of the war. "Christmas Legend 1943," a puppet play that she and her fellow fugitives performed, is one of her earliest surviving writings.

After her return to Germany in 1947, Grete Weil successfully sued to have the small pharmaceutical company that had been taken from her husband's family restored to its rightful owners. She remarried and turned to writing again, providing the libretto for Hans Werner Henze's *Boulevard Solitude* and translating works by Lawrence Durrell and John Hawkes. She published her first novel *The Last Trolley from Beethovenstraat* in 1963, followed by short stories and the novels *My Sister Antigone* in 1980 and *Generations* in

1983. Her final novel *The Bride Price* (1988) was awarded the Scholl prize, named for the sister and brother executed by the Nazis for their role in the resistance. *Aftershocks*, a collection of short stories, appeared in 1992, and in 1998 she published her memoirs, *Leb ich denn, wenn andere leben* ("I Live, When Others Live"). Grete Weil died at her home near Munich in 1999.